PRINTHOUSE BOOKS
PRESENTS

ZOE POUND
Haitians Formation

Miami's Urban Chronicles: Volume II

Thomas Barr Jr.

VIP INK PUBLISHING GROUP, INC.

Copyright, 2023 by Thomas Barr Jr.

PrintHouse Books, Atlanta, GA.   *published 4-15-2023*

www.PrintHouseBooks.com

VIP INK Publishing Group, Incorporated

This novel is fiction but also has been inspired by true events, most characters are fictitious no matter how true the event. Some characters remained the same as the events have been documented to the public and are on public record.

Cover art, designed by SK7

Paperback. ISBN – 979-8-3507-0655-0

Library of Congress Cataloging-in-Publication Data

ZOE POUND CHAPTER CONTENTS

Chapter 1 - Influxes

Chapter 2 - Oddities

Chapter 3 - Modifications

Chapter 4 - Associates

Chapter 5 - Knowledge

Chapter 6 - Refinement

Chapter 7 - Equal

Chapter 8 - Pioneering

Chapter 9 - Rise

Chapter 10 - Shark

Chapter 11 - Passions

Chapter 12 - Extravagant

Chapter 13 - Barren

Chapter 14 - Boss

Chapter 15 - transcend

Chapter 16 - Seed

Chapter 17 - Deceit

Chapter 18 - Exile

An old man reels in worn sails from the center ship's mast and spits a wad of tobacco on the floorboard. He struggles to wind the wrench handle attached to the rail and it soon jams in place as the vessel slows. The moon light shines upon the rippling water of the ocean as the vessel nears port. City lights are visible positioned along the shores of mega metropolis.

"Fred, this old ass shit is stuck," the man yells.

A woman walks over to the old man with a spray bottle containing a solution and sprays the handle. The man grunts as he's able to slowly wind the handle pulling the sails in and onto an extended rail. He grabs the mid-section of his pants bending over groaning in pain as the woman walks away from him.

"You're going to get ruptured yanking on that thing like that," she replied.

Terry Mack snickered and grinned as he watched the interaction between the two boat mates. He had been aboard for months and at ten years old was bored to death with the travel. He envisioned what his new life would be like in the United States. He traveled with his mother who had escaped from the detainment camps of Papa Doc, the ruthless Haitian president. Terry's father was a political prisoner of Francois "Papa Doc" Duvalier. He was locked up for questioning Duvalier's policy of social spending and public welfare.

"Bitch, give me that spray bottle and you bring in the sails from now on," the old man spat.

"Fuck you," she replied. "Your baby making factory has been foreclosed on for years."

Laughter could be heard as the two went back and forth insulting each other. Terry stood on the deck looking toward the dark shoreline. He could see flickering lights and he imagined what people were doing at that moment. The boat contained a few passengers who were lounging on the lower deck. Many were seasick from the long ocean voyage, but Terry was eager to reach his destination. His mother had family in Miami, and this was going to be the new start for her and Terry.

The ship hands moved about the boat preparing it to dock when there was a sudden jerking motion felt on the starboard bow.

A crashing sound could be heard as the boat took on water.

"Damn we hit a reef," the old man screamed.

The woman yanked open a nearby crate which contained life vests and passengers filed out of the lower deck to see what was going on. A much larger vessel was a few yards ahead and it was believed to be a Cuban cutter with migrants aboard. Unfortunately they were not aware of the trailing vessel's mishap and had already unloaded their passengers. The passengers aboard Terry's boat began jumping in the water to swim to dry land. Terry and his mother also leapt into the icy waters to make land. In the midst of the chaos, the US Coast Guard were alerted and were canvassing the location for the damaged vessel.

The crew and passengers of the boat were well aware of the wet foot dry foot policies of the United States. If a Haitian was caught they would truly be sent back to the island to face the murderous and deadly Papa Doc regime. If Cubans or any other nationality were caught they could remain on account of political refugee status.

It was good fortune that the island of Haiti was a

landmass which provided good swim holes for those who

cherished the outdoors. Terry had learned to swim as a

young lad and was quite a strong swimmer. His mother

was a swimmer as well. They were not far from the shore,

and they swam quietly in the night toward the city lights.

Terry's mother knew once they reached shore they had to

avoid the authorities and make contact with the family.

She swam with the purpose and direction for a discrete

spot to avoid detection. Terry could taste the salty sea

water as he paced himself alongside his mother. He swam

hard to keep up with her despite his short strokes which

forced him to swim at a faster pace. They soon made

landfall in no time and hit the beach running along with

other migrants. They had successfully avoided Coast

Guard detection and would phone relatives notifying them

for pickup.

Months earlier Terry's mother was approached by a man offering secret transport to the United States for a fee of $5,000 dollars per person. Terry's mother considered the offer because of her imprisoned husband. She knew her family was at risk of prosecution from the Haitian government. She and her son could face imprisonment or reprisal at any time. She couldn't bear living under such a condition and the anxiety of the situation was too heavy.

Terry's family was prominent in Haiti and had hailed from West Africa during post-colonial Haiti. During slavery days, the wealthy planters were at the top of the social class, but after the slave revolution and subsequent independence, Haiti's military class, mulattos, and free blacks made up the upper class. His progenitors had worked as indentured servants upon slave ships acting in the role of interpreters for slave catchers. They since rose through the social order taking over in farming land after the war. Terry's paternal family infiltrated the government order, and his father was from family of government officials.

Raising the capital to make the trip to America was not a major deal for his mother. She was largely concerned for the safety of her son. She would find a way to get word to her imprisoned husband of their planned departure to a new life. As many in the Haitian community could relate and were familiar with the instability of the island's politics.

There were many groups that participated in immigrant smuggling, and the ring that approached Terry's mother, worked out of a travel agency. All the logistics for the trip were pre-arranged and the funds were paid upon voyage cast off. The designated meeting points for loading the boat at the designated dock was secretly relayed by a courier. They would meet up with other parties to secure space in a sailing boat designated as the Sankofa. The Sankofa was a mythological bird which carried news of slaves back to Africa. Such was that of oral storytelling among West African descents. Terry and his mother would slip the shackles of the politically cursed land and endure an 800-mile trip to the United States.

Terry now sat in a small living room of his uncle's home as his mom and other adults held a conversation in the kitchen. Terry's uncle was a teacher who was exiled from Haiti in the late 1950s by the Duvalier government. He had been living in Miami for years and owned his own home. He worked as taxi driver in North Miami.

"You're lucky to be alive little sister." Terry heard his uncle say.

"Yeah, me and my baby had to swim nearly a mile to shore," replied Terry's mother.

"You better count your blessings that there were not sharks in the water," Terry's uncle said.

Terry had not considered the fact that they could've

been eaten by sharks. He was so concentrated on making it

to shore that the thought never entered his mind. He was

intently fixated on keeping pace with his mom which

consumed his thoughts completely.

"Yeah my little man was with me stroke for stroke,"

said Terry's mom.

Terry smiled to himself as he listened to the

conversation. He had counted on his quick strokes and his

strong swim style while in the water. Terry was also a

fierce competitor, and he felt the challenge of the swim in

some way decided his fate in this new country.

"Well he's just like his pops, likes to make a point,"

said the uncle.

"As soon as we hit the shore we took cover behind a

motel in the parking lot," said Terry's mom.

"Well, on late nights during the week those lots are

usually empty," replied the uncle.

"I was expecting your call sooner, I was beginning to worry," he said.

Terry could hear cups and saucers clinging as the adults talked. It was early morning and the smell of coffee lingered in the air. As he slumped in the sofa he felt his stomach churn from hunger, and he placed his hand over it. From all the excitement he had neglected food or drink and was now exhausted. His adrenaline was in overdrive and being in foreign surroundings gave him a weird type of vibe. He was afraid to sleep because he might've missed something, and he didn't necessarily want to eat because of anxiety. Sleep however crept in, and he snoozed silently as the adults chatted in the kitchen.

Terry's mother found work as a maid in guest services at the Fountainebleau Hotel on Miami Beach. She would catch public transportation at daybreak in order to be to work on time. The buses ran from early morning into late nights from the beach. Terry was the only child, so he often was home alone while his mother made a living. Working as an undocumented immigrant she soon earned enough money to rent a house in Miami Shores. Terry was entered into 5th grade at Little Edison Park Elementary School to begin his public education in the United States.

Terry often inquired about his father, however his mother rarely spoke of him. Terry would often hear her come home from work on late nights. She would routinely prepare her nightly supper and sob quietly at the table. He surmised she was gravely concerned about his father and pondered his fate in Haiti. Terry had heard his uncle talk of the man, and Terry's father was a military officer in Duvalier's government, who was declared a communist sympathizer. Duvalier had successfully supplanted the previous mulatto elites and was marshalling his own elite party of Afro-Haitians. Rural folks supported the regime while others were labeled communists he would hear his uncle say. Terry would often hear his uncle refer to the Haitian leader as the black dog killer.

It was believed that one of Duvalier's enemies had the power of shape shifting and could shift himself into a black dog. Duvalier decreed the killing of any black dog found in the country in an attempt to vanquish his enemy.

The neighborhood was located in a quaint part of town which was considered middle class for some of the Haitian immigrants. The poorer Haitians were from adeyo or the countryside. A few were urban dwellers from the poor sections of Port-au-Prince who mostly resided in the Little River area of Miami. Terry was curious of his neighborhood, and he explored his new surroundings every chance he got.

Terry's uncle purchased a bike for him as he knew the boy was new to the country and had limited transportation. Having a bike in the neighborhood was a big issue and was the first thing any kid got as it relates to toys. Terry never owned a bicycle, and he was thrilled to have finally possessed one in his new environment.

"You be careful with that and stay out the street," said Terry's uncle.

"Thanks a million, Uncle," Terry replied in an excited voice.

"It's dangerous out here and you have drivers on the road from all cultures," he said.

The streets of Miami were like a tropical jungle, and anything could happen at any given time or place. Terry's uncle was well aware of the inconsistencies in regard to the streets and Terry would learn this fact sooner than he expected.

"They have different attitudes and approach driving in various mindsets," he stated.

Terry hopped on his bike and sped down the street toward the basketball courts. He wanted to see the sights and explore the surroundings of the area. There were a few kids milling around the courts shooting basketballs. The older kids rode motor bikes and drove cars with loudspeaker sound systems that thumped with bass. The music from the cars was loud and the words rhymed over the thudding drumbeats. This was Terry's introduction to rap music, as this was not the culture of Haitian music, and it sounded strange.

Many of the vehicles were convertible cars and Chevy Impalas with candy painted color spray jobs. The cars were very clean and flamboyant. They were very different from the older run-down foreign vehicles of his old country. It seemed to Terry that everything was brighter and newer in this new country of America. The sun shone with a more vibrant nature, and this added to the appeal of being in the United States. This was a fresh start and Terry looked forward to the process with zeal and enthusiasm. He would become an American.

Chapter 2

The bell rang at Little Edison Park Elementary,

signaling the beginning of school, and Terry rambled down

the hallway in an attempt to find his class. His parents

continually expressed the importance of an American

education in the household, and he dreaded going to school.

Being a member of an immigrant class made one a target of

all sorts of indignities. Terry hated being the butt of jokes

by the American bullies in his class. It was hard being a

black immigrant in South Florida from a group negatively

and unfairly stereotyped.

Terry's teachers were a mix of Haitian American citizens and African American professionals. Most understood the predicament of the immigrant populations and worked hard to lessen the gap in regard to educational learning. As Terry took a seat in class to begin his sojourn in the public school system he noted the diversity surrounding him in his new class. There were Latin immigrants as well as African Americans in his new environment.

"Aston," the teacher quipped. "Here," replied the student.

"Miguel," the teacher continued. "Present," said the young man.

"Terry," said the teacher. "Here," he replied.

The roll call went on as Terry noted the names of his new classmates. Terry knew that in order for him to survive he needed allies. He would choose his friends from this lot of students and potentially build long term relationships throughout his public-school experience.

Terry met Jean Carter in his first year of public school as a new American immigrant. Jean was an immigrant as well and his family had come from the south countryside of Haiti. Jean's family had arrived in the country in an earlier wave period than Terry's family. Jean was a class clown and was often engaging with black Americans in telling momma jokes during class. Jean would come to the aid of immigrants who would often get bullied by repelling attackers with degrading accusatory jokes.

Terry and Jean became fast friends as they could relate culturally as brothers in the struggle against African American assailants. Jean was a lanky youngster interested in sports and flirting with the young female companions of his grade. Terry liked Jean's slick talk style and his ability to fast talk his way out of tight situations.

Terry also became friends with Benny Pierre who was a native-born Haitian whose family have been in the states for ages. Benny was a big kid with a solid muscled built frame who was into weightlifting and working out. Terry admired his strength, and his presence was well known when he stepped in a room full of people. Benny had a penetrating smile and quick wit about himself. He was a well-read person and knew a little about everything.

Jay Frank was the last of the friends and was befriended by Terry. He was an American born Haitian and a Dade county resident. His dad was from Port-au-Prince and his mom was born in Carol City. They were professionals who were well known in the community. Jay was a cerebral fellow with a keen mind for problem solving. He was slight in his build but very athletic. Jay's mom was from the Afro-Hispanic culture, so he was raised in a tri-lingual household.

Terry and his friends sat around a table as they ate during lunch period. School lunch time was the part of school he enjoyed. There was such a wide variety of American delicacies and he especially liked hamburgers.

"Hey, you want that," replied a fat kid as he pointed his finger into Terry's lunch tray.

The kid had approached the boys unseen and was now touching Terry's food with his bare hand. He possessed a huge smile across his pudgy face and his fellow classmates giggled as the exchange with Terry progressed.

"They say you Haitians eat cat and we don't serve that here," replied the fat faced African American kid.

The giggling classmates burst into laughter as the fat faced kid stood with his hand in Terry's lunch tray. Terry whirled and punched fat boy in his stomach and he fell back onto the floor. Jay, Jean, and Benny jumped on the kid and began stomping him. Terry watched his friends for a second and joined the ruckus.

"Don't let me get up, I'm gonna kill you," yelled the fat kid.

Terry could no longer hear the laughter and the jeers of the kids in the lunchroom as they stomped the kid. The fat kid slowly rose to his feet as he fought through the kicks of Terry's crew of friends. Apparently because of his size he was able to absorb the blows being rained down upon him. Terry suddenly saw the kid draw something from his pocket and flick his wrist as the object popped open.

"He got a blade," Terry yelled.

All the guys stopped and began backing away.

"I got you bastards now," said the fat kid.

His eyes had a sparkle in them as he swung in the air in a cutting motion toward his attackers. Terry could see fat boy was serious. He thought about making a grab for the knife in an attempt to wrestle it away from him. He paused and glanced over the faces of his friends. They seemed perplexed and he couldn't gauge if they were on his level of thought. As the fat kid continued to threaten the crew with the open blade someone stepped from the crowd. A cold barrel poked the fat boy in the back of the head.

"Drop it," replied the person.

Terry recognized the person with the gun as Aston. He gripped a 9mm Glock. Aston was his African American classmate and sat a seat over from him in his home room class. Fat boy instantly dropped the knife as he knew exactly what the object was to his head. Gun play meant many things in a street fight, and most of all, it meant you were a major player if you possessed one.

"You guys better get lost," he said as he motioned toward Terry.

Terry and his friends had cut class. They made their way over to Washington Park to hang out at the b-ball courts. The b-ball courts were a place where many of the older neighborhood young adults hung out. Gang members from various neighborhoods associated around the b-ball courts. Gangs such as One Way, Uptown, Sesame Street, E-Unit and Zombie Boys.

"I'm tired of the immigrant jokes and these bullies," said Benny.

Terry eyed his friend for a minute and then turned to watch the older boys on the b-ball court as they engaged in hoops. Pierre and Jay nodded their head in agreement and sat on the nearby bleachers to watch the action. Cars were parked in a nearby parking lot with loud bass, booty shaking, music playing. It was hard owning up to being Haitian and many kids try to just pass as American by not acknowledging their background. Terry knew many such people, but he however would never consider this approach.

"Yeah, that Aston kid pulled a strap on fat boy," remarked Jay.

"That kid was scared as hell too," said Jean.

Terry silently watched the game on the b-ball court as the guys chatted. He knew their problems were just beginning. He was surprised Aston stuck his neck out the way he did in order to help them out. He wondered what the catch was. Aston was an American, an African American. Why would he go out on a limb for us in that way? Jean voiced the thought Terry pondered about.

"Why would Aston pull a gun on fat boy," Jean inquired.

"Who gives a fuck," replied Benny.

"I was getting ready to take that blade from him and whip his ass," said Benny.

"I think we owe Aston," said Terry.

"Yeah," replied Jay.

It was well known that many African Americans participated in bullying newly arrived immigrants in the community. Many immigrants simply ignored the problem, and few publicly spoke about the issue. The tactic was to just ignore the matter and hope that it would die down dissipating into oblivion.

There was a story told to new immigrants about maintaining cultural pride and becoming successful in the American society. The story of Phede was about a twelve-year-old boy who arrived in Miami from Haiti and quickly assimilated. He began to "cover-up," hiding his Haitian identity by Americanizing his name to Fred. He would speak English without an accent and never speak Creole, not even at his home. He grew into a teenager, had a job at McDonald's, sang in the Baptist choir, became an honor student in school and hoped to be a doctor one day.

One day, Fred's girlfriend, an African American, came to visit during his break at the restaurant. While they were talking, Fred's sister arrived and spoke to him in Creole. She blew his cover, and he blew his cool. Fred screamed at her to never speak Creole to him again. He didn't want to be known as a Haitian. Four days later, the young man bought a .22 caliber revolver for fifty dollars. He went to an empty lot near his home and killed himself with a bullet to his chest.

The moral of the story was to maintain your cultural heritage. The young man aimed to gain acceptance in the predominantly African American neighborhood where he lived, attended school, and church. He tragically believed that covering up his national heritage, dating African American girls and speaking the African American vernacular was his only possible path to success.

Terry was well aware of his predicament, and he was a goal-oriented person with pride in who he was as an individual. He felt it as unfair for his people to be treated differently because of the way they lived and viewed life. He felt that everyone should be given a fair chance at becoming a success in society and providing for their own. He contemplated ways of countering the bullying and harassment by African Americans. He came to the idea of mastering their culture and immolating it to push the

Haitian American agenda.

Chapter 3

"Get up Terry, time for school," said Terry's mom.

She flicked the light switch on in Terry's room.

"I told you about hanging out late," she said. "You need your rest."

Terry pulled the cover over his eyes to shield them from the light. He despised getting up early during the mornings. He loved the relaxing slumber of sleep, and he especially enjoyed it when he was required to get up. He could hear his mother rummaging around his room, and he wondered what she was looking for.

"Breakfast is in the fridge," she said. "You know how to use the microwave."

She left the room light on as she walked through the house. Terry could hear her voice trail off as she prepared for her job at Foutainbleau. He knew she had to be on time for the bus to travel across the bridge for work. She made sure every morning to wake him before she departed for the day. He appreciated this gesture, but he would make the best of his day learning to become an American.

"Get up Terry," she replied.

He heard the door slam as she departed. He slung

his feet to the floor and scanned his room to see if anything

was out of place. Terry was aware of his mother's curiosity

and would have to be watchful in concealing his personal

items from her random inspections. He dressed, prepared

his breakfast, and was out the door for school within the

hour. After school he hit the neighborhood in search of an

afterschool job. Being a latch key kid Terry barely saw his

mother during her work week and during her time off she

slept most of the time.

Many of the immigrant kids were unable to get jobs

in grocery store chains and even with the fast-food chains.

Word of mouth was the docks were a good place to make

big money under the table and work for unlimited number

of hours. Terry would hang around the docks and visit

local longshore men hall meetings.

He would attempt to gain all the knowledge he could attain in regard to finding a way to make tangible big money.

"Say young blood, you looking for work?" inquired a passing stranger.

Terry had been hanging around the downtown longshore men's hall one Saturday and many of the staff were familiar with him being about.

"Yes sir," replied Terry.

The man looked as if he had just completed labor intensive work. He was dressed in a dingy white shirt with work pants. It was a breezy day, and the sun was bright in the sky. People were sparingly entering and exiting the building while Terry was mingling near the sidewalk walkway.

"See the receptionist inside, ask for a Twic card application," the stranger said.

He produced a business card that read, "A-man semi driver."

The man continued down the sidewalk as Terry was left holding the card. He immediately proceeded in the building to contact the receptionist. She coordinated with Terry for him to obtain a Twic card and soon after he was employed as a part time stevedore aka "Lasher" on the docks.

Working on the port proved to be back breaking work for a youth and Terry worked hard on the job. Most of his spare time went to hanging out on the dock trying to get all the work that presented itself to him. Terry's mother believed work was a good thing for him because she was of the opinion that this kept him from the streets.

"Yo, man what you doing out here?" Terry heard someone say.

He realized it was Aston. As Aston approached him he realized he was in work gear complete with goggles and work gloves.

"I work here," replied Terry.

"So do I," said Aston.

"Cool," said Terry.

Terry and Aston worked on various ships unloading and stocking docked ships in their off time after school. As they worked together on different jobs they soon realized mutual interests. Terry loved working long extra hours for more money. Aston enjoyed making money as well and often they would chat about top-of-the-line cars and flashy cigarette boats.

Aston lived in the Carol City section of Miami which was a middle class African American neighborhood. Terry soon started hanging out with Aston after work and grew to admire his lifestyle. As an American black the culture was vastly different from that of Haitians. Blacks were more enthralled in this Capitalist society than Haitians. Aston's older brother was a long-time drug dealer in the area. He was well known and always drove new cars. Aston's brother would sometimes drive the two to work and Terry was impressed with him.

"Man I wish I could drive a car like this," said Terry.

"We could do it with hard work," replied Aston.

"You mean smart work," said Hollywood.

Hollywood wore a closely cropped hair style and always dressed in linen outfits. This gave him a relaxed and carefree swag. He appeared free of the everyday pressures of working for folks punching a clock. He was not working for the man but working the system perpetuated by the man. He was always smiling with his top row of gold teeth glittering in the sunlight.

"Smart work is work without breaking your back," said Hollywood.

The years passed as the two boys worked on the docks and grade school and junior high soon translated to high school. As the boys grew into teenagers, money became the paramount motivator in all things. Hollywood had developed into a major pusher in Miami and Terry had soaked up much of his lessons as a player in the streets. Aston passed along information of drug smuggling at the port to Terry

and they soon were proficient at identifying ships with dope.

Jean, Benny, and Jay Frank soon began robbing docked ships of their drug shipments for the purpose of selling them on the streets for profit. Terry acquired guns from Aston, who in turn would get them from his brother's friends. Armed with Glock 45s and AK Choppers they would sweep through the port under the cover of night surprising snoozing crew members robbing them blind. Terry's knowledge of port operations was unparalleled. He knew where ships from Haiti and Colombia were usually docked, and shore time leave hours of ship's crew members. He also was aware of the area customs agents and all other security movements of the port.

"Benny get down," said Terry.

Terry, Jean, Jay Frank, and Benny lay prone along a perimeter fence line outside of a docked transport ship. Lights flashed along the top of the fence and moved down the fence line toward an adjacent cargo ship. It was pitch black along the canal sidewalks that ran parallel to the ship's main docking doorways. They crept down the fence and slipped into a darkened doorway onto the bay area of a docked ship.

"Check the cargo boxes," said Terry.

The ship's hallway was darkened with shadows as Terry directed the crew of robbers down into the hull of the boat. Terry remained on the bay of the ship to scope for security. He could hear the guys cock their AK Choppers as they made their way to the bottom.

The men raffled through the cargo boxes and returned to the bay of the ship with three duffle bags full of kilos of white powered cocaine. Terry placed the Glock 45 he had on safety and slung one of the bags over his shoulder. He buckled a little and was amazed at the heaviness of the bag he carried. He had accurately calculated the leave time of the ship's crew and they avoided all on duty security for that post. The men crept down the ramp off the ship and headed for the getaway vehicle. Spotlights continued to crisscross the sky in search of any potential intruders unbeknown of the fleeing men in dark apparel.

Terry and his crew acquired forty kilos of cocaine in the shipyard heist at the port. The going rate for one kilo of cocaine was $35,000 on the streets. Terry and his crew sold off much of the cocaine wholesale to Hollywood.

Hollywood and his crew in Carol City then sold them off in grams and bags to lesser dealers throughout the city. Grams usually ran about $50 t0 $80 dollars depending on the purity of the product.

Terry met up with the guys at the courts in the hood. It was a hot sunny day, and a wicked game of basketball was going on at the courts. Young men ran hastily battling to block basketball shots and shoving for a place to rebound the ball.

"What's the split on the loot," asked Benny.

"Half," said Jean.

"I don't think so, we need to reinvest some of the take for something viable," said Terry.

"I agree," replied Jay Frank.

"Let's start a car club," said Benny. "We can call it Zoe Pound."

"Zoe Pound," said Jean.

"Zoe Pound sounds kind of dope," said Jean.

"Everybody agree," asked Terry.

"I think so," replied Jay Frank. "Let's do it."

Terry divided some of the take with the crew and invested the rest in vintage old muscle cars. The cars mostly acquired were the 1978 Chevy Impalas and a one Chevy Caprice. They were personally detailed and upgraded for car shows. Most car shows took place on the weekend and occurred throughout various parts of the city. Many dope boys and pushers put their money up betting in car racing. Some placed bets on who had the most bass in the car audio systems. Competition became fierce on the streets in displaying the wealth of hustle money.

Chapter 4

Terry went about the task of organizing the car club business and he conducted research to find out how to get it started. He considered the Hell's Angels motorcycle organization and decided to structure it in that manner. The crew originally agreed on the group name of Zoe Pound for the car club and the mission would be the capitalist agenda of making and flaunting money.

Terry met up with the crew at Lake Lucerne basketball courts which was the childhood courts of the group since grade school. The location would later become the rallying location for the car club gatherings for events.

"Man I sold 20 grams this week fucking around on 51st Street," said Benny.

"How much did you make," asked Jean.

"Almost $200 dollars," replied Benny.

"Stupid don't be selling that shit yourself," said Terry.

"Yeah fool, get one of them young boys to do that shit," said Jay Frank.

"They get less time when they get caught by the pigs," said Terry.

The basketball courts were empty, and the guys had parked their cars in a semi-circle near the back entrance of Washington Park. Benny drove a box Chevy Impala with a candy apple red paint job with Vogue tires. Jean drove a green, big body, convertible, Chevy Impala with chrome hammer rims and a peanut butter color leather seats with the dash. Jay Frank drove a black Chevy Impala with limo tint windows and wide race car tires. Terry drove a baby blue Chevy Caprice with Truz and Vogue tires with all white leather seats and dash.

"Are we going to school today?" inquired Benny.

"I know I am," said Terry. "My mom's riding my ass."

"I'm with you," replied Jay Frank.

"Fuck that," replied Benny. "Jean let's go to the strip club."

"Cool, let's hit it," said Jean.

Terry was a senior at Edison High School, and he maintained good grades despite what other people thought of him in the streets. His mother was a stickler for education and was always on him as an immigrant in the importance of an American education. He maintained decent grades to keep her off his back in order to do his business in the streets. She has grown weary in her work in the hotel industry, and he wanted to be in position to help her later in life. After school he headed over to Carol City to check on Aston. He parked his Chevy Caprice in the park across the street from Aston's house. Aston's sister Sheryl approached him as he got out the car.

"Hello Terry," said Sheryl. "Nice car."

"You like?" replied Terry. "When are you going to let me take you out?"

"When you ask," replied Sheryl.

"I'm asking now," said Terry.

Sheryl was a beautiful, cocoa complexioned, thick thighed, girl with a bob cut hairstyle. She was the tall athletic built younger sister of Aston. Terry was very smitten by the girl's beauty, and she was fond of him as well. Sheryl was a year younger than Terry, but she would always help him with his schoolwork. The two walked across the street and encountered Aston standing on the front of the house.

"What's up Terry," said Aston. "My brother needs to meet with you 'bout some business."

"Ok, cool," replied Terry.

"See you soon, Beautiful," said Terry to Sheryl.

She walked past the two and entered the house. Terry and Aston walked up the street to meet Hollywood. He was at the pool room he owned where he held court with his runners. Many of the low-level dealers from the neighborhood hung at the spot. It was a local mini mart that sold odds and ends in small quantities. It was one of the few investments Hollywood made in his neighborhood by purchasing property.

"What's good Terry, I need another shipment," said Hollywood.

"I'll have to get back to you," replied Terry.

Terry could tell Hollywood was uneasy. He sat on a stool fiddling with a pool stick. Other guys were shooting pool and rolling dice. On occasion, in the streets, there is a period when certain drugs are hard to find. In this instance it seemed Terry's runners and pushers were low on that grade A Columbian cocaine. It was known in the streets that Zoe Pound dealt with high quality dope and the Zoes gave a lot for the money.

"Hey, I know you get updates from the brothers in Haiti on shipments," said Hollywood.

"Man why you trying to put me out there," replied Terry. "Just hold on, I got you."

"I'm playing with you, man," said Hollywood. "But get at me homeboy."

Terry had built a viable relationship with Aston and his brother Hollywood. He greatly benefited from his association with them. So he wanted to ensure he kept the relationship on good terms, and he would usually give a favorable buy rate on any and all products. When the next shipment comes in he would make sure to give Hollywood a good rate for whatever amount. Terry made good money from the last shipped load and made decent investments with his money. His street runners in the little Haiti neighborhood kept a steady influx of cash filling his pockets. The crew was greatly invested in fixing up their vehicles for the car shows and tricking off their money at the strip clubs. It seemed they spent money as fast as it was made. However Terry was more frugal and had his eyes on a much larger prize than most.

Terry assembled the crew at Washington Park located down from the Lake Lucerne basketball courts. It was a Friday night and the courts was filled with the neighborhood guys playing basketball. Others hung around the courts enjoying the games and making side bets on the game winner. A few were gathered off court rolling dice. Terry occasionally rolled dice when he had the extra cash for a quick hustle. He enjoyed the comradery associated with playing the game. He liked to let the guys know that he was one of them. He was from the hood, and he represented it to the fullest in his true street bravado way.

Terry snatched up the pair of dice from the floor as the last person rolled crapped out.

"I'm getting in on this roll," he said.

He took a hundred-dollar bill from his pocket and placed it on the sidewalk. The group gathered began making side bets on the game. Benny placed a hundred-dollar bill on the ground indicating he was up next to roll the dice. Terry rattled the dice in his hand violently and blew his breath on the dice. He slung the dice from his hand onto the sidewalk.

"Seven or eleven baby," he yelled.

The two cubes rolled to a stop. The crowd of men yelled, and Benny slumped to his knees. Terry had rolled an eleven. Rolling a seven or eleven is an instant win in street corner dice and Terry won without even giving Benny a chance to roll the dice.

"Run it back," exclaimed Benny.

He slapped down another hundred-dollar bill on the concrete and Terry met the bet with one of the hundreds he'd previously won. Benny grabbed up the dice and shook it within his closed fist. He then let it fly from his hand on to the sidewalk. The dice hit the ground and rolled out the number three. Rolling a three was an automatic loss in Craps.

"Crap," said Terry.

Terry grabbed up the money and the group of men exchanged dollars on their side bets made on the game. Benny was down two hundred bucks within the span of seconds and his luck looked bleak in the face of Terry's winning streak. He shrugged his shoulders in defeat and conceded the game. Dice could mean trouble with the volatile mix of money and tempers. In many neighborhoods throughout the city pickup games of craps have been an entertainment staple for decades. "If they didn't like each other, one of them would be dead right now," said one of the side betters, half-jokingly.

Benny was visibly frustrated with his loss and was ready to make some real money from the take on the streets.

"It's Friday night and I'm trying to get paid," said Benny.

Terry took from his pocket a hand full of gold medallions and tossed them to Benny.

"Put this on," he said.

Benny took the medallions and quickly slipped one on as he passed them around the group. He seemed to know exactly what they were. As many Haitians used medallions and small crafted figures of saints for protection. Terry would use any means necessary in order to pull off successful heists on the port.

"We're going to hit a big boat tonight," said Terry.

"Yeah we got all the protection we need now," stated Benny.

Jean and Jay Frank put the medallions on and pushed them down under their shirts. They respected the power of Voodoo but feared it. In the streets any and every power was called upon to avoid trouble. Many street cats told stories of being invisible to cops during drug search and seizures in the hood. It was not known how true the stories were, but they served as inspirations to incorporate in illicit activities.

Terry anxiously waited at the park in preparation for ripping off the next drug shipment at the dock. They planned to move after midnight and being seen near the courts down from the park was cover. The games on Friday night often lasted to early morning as groups played hours at a time. The guys seemed bored as they prepped for the feat.

"Man, let's hit up a strip club," said Benny.

"Are you crazy," replied Jay Frank. "We need to stay sharp."

"Yeah, we got a lot riding on this take," said Terry.

Chapter 5

Terry met Sheryl for their date out on South Beach.

He had his car detailed at Carol City's top auto detail shop.

In Carol City, washing automobiles by hand was the most

thorough approach to getting a good detail. Terry was very

concerned about not damaging the paint on his car. Most

guys who had cars in car shows were very cautious of auto

paint damage from automatic car wash places. The best

method was a good hand wash removing all the dirt from

the paint. Soapy water to wash the surface and then a good

rinse. The use of a chamois leather cloth was often used to

dry the surface with no streaks.

Upon viewing the freshly detailed car, Sheryl's

mouth dropped. She could not believe how clean and new

the vehicle looked. Young cats in the hood were impressed

by fine cars, cloths, hoes, and money. It seemed only the

dope boys and preachers were the ones with money. Every

move made by the major players were watched closely by many. From the Jordans, fitted hats, Girbauds, Solja Reeboks, Ferrari cars, herringbone jewelry, big body cars, to the classic Chevys.

"Just so you know, I like you regardless of what people say," said Sheryl.

"What do people say?" inquired Terry.

"Well my brother says you're greedy," said Sheryl. "He believes you undercut him on deals."

"I can't believe he tells you this shit," replied Terry.

Terry didn't appreciate the fact that Hollywood was telling his business to other people especially to his sister. Terry took this as a question of the man's integrity. In a way Terry took this act as dry snitching. He knew from this point on that Hollywood could not be trusted and he would need to be on guard.

"Let's go to Wet-n-Willie," said Sheryl.

"Fine," replied Terry.

Terry was immersed in his thoughts as he drove to South Beach and almost forgot about his rider in the car.

It was only days before Terry had completed the ship heist with the crew and had made the deal for forty keys with Hollywood. Hollywood pressed him all week for the shipment and seemed desperate. Terry had gotten the impression that he may have took a lost on the street from one of his workers. It was known that some street hustlers would substitute a brick of flower for the real dope. They then would pocket the real stuff and resell it for a profit on another block. Terry heard all the rip off stories of street life and wasn't surprised. Hollywood could be shrewd at times and his prickly personality won him few friends. He was arrogant but Terry dealt with him on the strength of his brother. Working with Aston on the docks was an invaluable experience. His current position in the hustle game was owed to that experience.

Terry continued to date Hollywood's sister, however he was growing uncomfortable with him. He could not put a finger on it but something inside his soul was telling him something wasn't right. Terry believed in a street code and with the dismantling of the cocaine cartels in the city there was lawlessness on the streets. Replaced with the inner-city gangsters, everyone was going for self. Terry realized the key to surviving and prospering in the street was organization. He would seek to build a comradery among his crew which would be unbreakable.

Terry thought of many ways to unite his crew and he thought of one thing they had in common. Many gang members in the neighborhood didn't have a male figure in the house. They had fathers, but no male presence that influenced their lives. Many of the guys he knew were void of any type of brotherhood outside of friendly basketball pickup games in the park. He was familiar with the Boy Scouts and other church groups in the community. The guys he knew could not afford to participate in these

functions as kids nor had the transportation to. They often

learned to just deal with surface-level interaction and

solitude as men. He did realize when he was with his

friends doing fun and interesting things, they were happy.

Having a relationship seemed to empower them to perform

at the highest level. They competed among each other

which brought out the best.

Terry setup the next heist on the port and the crew

congregated at a nearby dock from the ship. It was

midnight and the wind blew lightly over the waters. Terry

crept along the shoreline with his Glock cocked; he was

followed closely by Jean, Benny, and Jay Frank. They

were all strapped with automatic weapons. Jean clutched

an AK, Benny had his Chopper, and Jay Frank had a .45

with a laser. The lights were dimmed on the ship and the

deck hands were nowhere in sight. They slipped onto the

side of the ship by way of the extended walkway and

peered through one of the cloudy windows on the ship.

The crew moved in silence, and they were dressed

in all dark clothes. Their movements were swift and

deliberate. They charged onto the bridge of the ship and

took its crew at gunpoint.

"Where the dope at?" yelled Terry.

Jean cracked the officer of the watch on the head

with the butt of his weapon. Blood instantly squirted from

the side of the man's head as he fell. The other seaman saw

this and immediately began stammering the location of the

drugs. Jay Frank grabbed one of the seamen and he led

him down into the bow of the ship. Terry and Benny stood

guard over the other crewmen with weapons drawn ready

for action. Jay Frank loaded all the bricks of cocaine he

could carry, and they swiftly exit the ship.

Terry made it a point to preach to the crew about

not being greedy. Greed was often what led to many a

person's downfall. In the drug game it was hard to report crimes to law enforcement when you're dirty yourself. Terry's crew had made a large score on this take, and they needed to sell the keys and get cash fast. It was well known in the streets that drugs were becoming scarce. The Feds had been cracking down on the Cocaine Cowboys who ran rampant and unchecked throughout Dade County. So Terry could sell his supply of dope at a higher rate for more money. All the dealers in Carol City, if they were smart, could see this coming down the pipeline.

Little did Terry know Hollywood was well aware of this and he had deceitful plans of his own for profiting. Hollywood had heard about the heist Terry and the crew did. He sent word to Terry of a time and place for the buy. Terry usually made the deals with the assistance of Aston, but he was out of town, so he took Jay Frank with him.

They met up in the parking lot of a strip club called the Rolex. Hollywood had four of his goons with him.

They drove a black two door Cutlass with Vogue tires.

Terry and Jay Frank were in a rental with the bricks loaded

in back. Terry was suspicious of Hollywood because of the

words of his sister, so he was on guard. Terry decided to

try Hollywood, so he pulled up and then suddenly sped out

of the parking lot kicking up gravel as he went.

Hollywood's goons suddenly started shooting at the van as

it turned down the street and out of site. His suspicion was

right, and he now had a war on his hands with the African

American thugs.

     They pulled up in North Miami and parked down

from the local dope spot called the White House. The

White House was one of the main hustle spots in the

neighborhood which did volumes of business. The crew

was on hand, and they unloaded the bricks and prepared for

street distribution sales. They now needed cash for

weapons and ammunition. The word spread quickly on

what had occurred with Hollywood, and dealers were soon

choosing sides.

The bricks Terry was in possession of had translated

into money. He knew Hollywood would need another

supplier because the streets were drying up. It was difficult

to find a "connect" and Terry was the only player in town

that could touch those ships for that work. Haitians in

Miami were privy to what shipments the Colombians were

sending to the mainland. They had firsthand knowledge on

what they could rip off and how much they could get away

with. As the cartels allowed a certain amount to get lost or

confiscated by the cops. Terry's crew were well aware of

these unknown secrets. Hollywood indeed had put him and

his workers in a tough spot. Greed was the result in that

instance Terry thought to himself as he pondered the

situation. He wondered if Aston had a role in this

occurrence, but he was not sure. Aston had been a friend

for a long time, and he would hate to have this relationship damaged in anyway.

Terry decided to contact Sheryl and find out more of what her brother Hollywood was up to. He invited her out for drinks at a club called the Office and this club was located on the border of the North Miami/Carol City line. She showed up on the scene looking fly as ever with her tight-fitting Gucci jeans and classy high heels. Terry had reserved a back table for them, and he ordered her favorite food which awaited her at the table.

"Hello baby," said Terry. "How are you?"

Terry pulled out a chair from the table as she sat down.

"I should be asking you that, I heard what happened," she replied.

"Your brother is gone off the deep end," he said.

"Why is he making me an enemy?"

"The streets are drying up and he needs bread," she replied.

She sips a glass of Moet Chandon Dom Perignon Rose and pops a green grape in her mouth. She grimaces from the sourness of the grape. She takes another sip from her glass to offset the taste of the grape.

"What's his next move," Terry inquired.

"He knows about a couple of houses your guys use to stash drugs," she said. "He plans to home invade those houses."

Sheryl had just answered the question that was plaguing Terry. She confirmed her brother Aston's complicity with Hollywood's antics. No one knew of the stash houses used to store surplus drug loads from docked ships. No one knew of the Haitian gangsters that tipped off the American port workers of smuggled drugs who in turn passed it on to the streets for a fee. Aston was the person who had known of this because of his position at the port.

Terry and Aston formally worked together to build a distribution pipeline using his brother Hollywood as one of the main buyers. With dope drying up on the streets blood is obviously thicker than water thought Terry to himself.

Chapter 6

Terry met up with a few other dealers throughout Dade County and developed business arrangements for distribution deals. Terry was aware that Hollywood was out on his robbing spree jacking drug dealers. He prepared his crew and workers with arms plus ammunition to go to war with any gang from Carol City.

Terry needed guns, so he arranged to setup straw purchases of AK-47s, among other arms, from local pawn stores. He surveyed local college campuses and recruited grad students to pose as straw buyers for pre-selected automatic weapons. He would give them the money for the purchase and turn around and buy the weapons back from them.

With Hollywood preoccupied with robbing he left his territory wide open for other street level peddlers.

Terry flooded dope throughout the corridors of the community. He did business with midlevel and retail level distributors who developed open-air drug markets, sold in clubs, apartment buildings, motels, vehicles and on beaches.

Terry's crew began strictly pirating boats that smuggled Colombian cocaine. The Miami River was a waterway largely used by these vessels. The boats would slip down to private docks in the neighborhoods and unload the cargo without detection from law enforcement. Terry would pay well for information on shipments that were profitable to the crew. The Colombians soon began using Haitian vessels for smuggling which made it easier for Terry to rob.

Terry and his crew became proficient at pirating boats, ships and other vessels that were used by the smugglers. They developed crude practices for expunging information from vessel seaman on the docked ships. Folks lost ears, fingers, and certain body parts if they were not

forth coming in telling where dope was hidden. Smugglers

developed inventive ways for hiding drugs and contraband

on ships entering the country. They used products such as

coffee grains, baking soda, Petroleum Vaseline, and baby

powder.

They would often wrap the drugs in cans of coffee

grains which blunted the smell for the search hounds. They

were also fond of wrapping dope in plastic bags covering

the outer side with Petroleum Vaseline to be hid in the bulk

heads of ships.

The key in pirating docked ships on the waterway

was that of time. Terry had discovered the response time of

the average police unit in the city. One had to be in and out

before time was up, beating law enforcement's response

time. In most cases if they had effectively controlled the

seamen and all the mates, time was of no essence. In some

cases, violence had to be inflicted to coax people to follow orders. Often times the size of the ship dictated the sort of pirate tactic to implement. Usually on larger ships the crew liked to use the AKs. With smaller boats high caliber handguns could be used for better maneuverability.

The crew never identified a single leader of the clan, however the style of leadership was one of a committee rule type thing. Usually the one with the most knowledge of a situation could guide how things went. Terry made sure to be in the know for any and everything when it came to street hustling and robberies. Many of the other street gangs in Carol City were violent and brash in committing criminal offenses. Terry's crew only used violence when it was necessary for making money related moves. If they were identified by the detectives for ongoing investigations it was of no major consequence. They would simply change their names and develop another lifestyle to avoid detection. The culture of most gangs were, "I'm down for life." However, that was not the case with Zoe Pound. Zoe Pound's major concern was survival.

Terry held most of the cargo from the ship heists at the Zoe Pound stash house called the White House. The White House was the central location for Zoe Pound activities. They also maintained lesser-known stash houses throughout Miami. Whenever shipments came in the first stop likely would be the White House.   Terry had developed friendships with street level hustlers throughout the Carol City neighborhood. Cutting Hollywood from his list of contacts would not be a major issue. Although he was a major distributor who could sell off a lot of work quickly he was an expendable asset. He attracted so much drama and negativity until it was not worth the headache.

Terry would use the many street level peddlers to flush out the overabundance of dope to ready and waiting buyers. With scarcity, demand increased which resulted in increased profits. Terry knew the law of supply and demand. The quantity demanded is the amount of a product people are willing to buy at a certain price. The relationship between price and quantity demanded is known as the demand relationship. Supply represents how much the market can offer.

Terry became a master at coordinating his drug game. His mother didn't know he had given up work entirely. The money he made from dope allowed him to make major moves. He would tell his mom that the car show business kept him busy, but that was not the case. Terry would hustle all day when not jacking ships. He would wake up at 5am in the morning and go to sleep around midnight.

He made sure to supply his peddlers with the best product for the purpose of keeping customers loyal. The street peddlers were often young of age, and they could avoid being sentenced for long years. They would slang drugs to junkies and anyone with the money to get high.

Most of the peddlers smoked weed, gambled, and caroused at the local strip clubs.

Terry was now a young man, and he was done with school of any type. He had obtained a GED only to keep his mom off his back. He was more concerned with making the most money he could in the streets. Instead of advancing as a scholar he had advanced as a master's level player. He had dreamed of making it out of poverty and self-doubt. As a founding member of the Zoe Pound he realized the ability of power. He had earned more money than his ancestors put together. He desired to become more than just another black person with money. He desired to build a lasting legacy, but he had no idea on how to accomplish it.

He had learned that control was a perceived experience of being able to determine outcomes. He was able to make decisions and see the outcomes of his will through others. This gave him the impression of being able to control the outside world. He reasoned if he was able to

control his own thoughts, feeling and behavior that it was

possible to control his world. His world now was the world

of crime and drugs.

Terry invested most of the money he earned into

purchasing old, dilapidated houses in the neighborhood.

He used these houses as dwellings to warehouse his drugs,

cars, guns, and workers that worked on the streets. He had

stash houses everywhere and he used most of these places

as staging locations. From these places he strategized with

peddlers to dominate the drug game block by block. This

caused major upheaval in the streets which led to shoot outs

and drive-bys. Blood shed had become the norm in the

streets, and everyone was strapped with a weapon.

Terry's underlings began acquiring munitions on

their own at alarming rates. They acquired tactical gear

such as armor vests, police gear, and badges. They targeted

law enforcement vehicles and military installations for

robbery scenarios. They burglarized unmarked vehicles and National Guard armories throughout the county.

Terry's initial aspirations were not criminal in nature. In the beginning he desired only to be equal as every other person in the community. Being Haitian had proved to be a heavy cross to bear in America. The language and culture proved to separate his kind from other colored folks. He felt he was a Negro as any other American. The competitive nature of his peers, among other things, had driven him to what he now was. He felt he had to harden himself to others in order to do what was needed to be done. Many in the crew had joined because of different reasons. Fear, money, lack of jobs, protection, kinship, recreation, and excitement were all reasons which attracted the youth. Terry would learn to harness the power of the numbers of these youth to build something memorable.

The old gangsters in Haiti had proved beneficial in passing along information about ships loaded with illegal drugs. Many of the old gangsters started under the voodoo inspired zenglendos, which is Creole, meaning bandit. These old school Haitian gangsters operated in the color of night and preyed in the slums or working-class neighborhoods. They set the tone of violence for all Haitian gangsters to follow in criminal practices. That was the one thing which benefited the Zoe in comparison with other Miami hustle crews. Having foreign associations outside of the country gave the gang a certain power in the streets. Of course funds were kicked back to the old timers for their help. It was well worth it because this made them a success. Zoe Pound had access to dope when local law enforcement shut down the supply coming out of Cuba, Honduras, and Mexico. In Carol City and other neighborhoods this gave rise to the Jack boys. Drug dealers who are robbed and killed don't get much attention on the news or with law enforcement. Hollywood had become a Jack boy and because he was on bad terms with Terry his hustle was up.

Terry's relationship with Aston had soured and it was apparent he was on the side of his brother. However Aston was not the average street corner peddler. He was particular of who he conducted business with. He was not impressed with being the center of attention or a major boss. He was associated with the major drug connections. He facilitated the major shipment deals and was very familiar with Haitian and Columbian smuggling operations. He was Terry's partner in facilitating the major pirating deals early on and now could possibly pass information on to Hollywood. Terry decided to secure his relationship with Sheryl, and he would keep his enemy close.

Chapter 7

Terry and the Zoe Pound were known for their

muscle cars and attended car shows around Dade County.

As well as running dope in the streets, they were car

enthusiasts. They owned a variety of Buicks, Impalas,

Caprices, and convertible Cadillacs. In these car shows, the

crew expressed their creativity in upgrading cars. Candy

paint jobs, 30 spoke shiny wire rims and big chrome grills

were apart of making a car stand out in the streets. Many

of the cars pumped bass music with the back seats covered

with woofers. Terry's car had a trunk-rattling system in

which he battled other car systems for supremacy. Terry

enjoyed the car shows and Zoe Pound always represented

well in the show competitions. They displayed the wet

paint look with colors such as bright reds, greens, and blues

on their vehicles. What was popular to see on cars in Carol

City were the Vogue tires with white-wall and the gold stripes.

Most of the shows occurred in the parks or a long strips near the beach. Many of the other car clubs would compete with the Zoe Pound in decorating the interior of their cars with Gucci. Custom steering wheels, gear shifters with matching dashboards, and interiors were eye catching. The head turner was the custom leather seats or even the fur interior. Terry also enjoyed the many creative coordinations done by competitors in engine upgrades. Chrome plating the Chevy small block V8, and chrome plating tailpipes added a subtle unforeseen power to a muscle car. In addition to displaying the looks of the cars many of the clubs raced the cars.

The outings also attracted many of the drug dealers, street players, pimps, prostitutes, and numbers runners. Barbeque grills were everywhere with people selling ribs, chicken, and other ethnic foods. The smell of smoke from the grills could be detected for miles and the bass music

from cars thumped mercilessly. Terry appreciated the

crowds that attended the shows, and he was acknowledged

for the work he had put into upgrading his car. The Zoe

Pound garnered much respect in the streets from these type

of American events. He could now see that he had come a

long way to improving the view that black Americans had

of his people. However, he still felt he had more to prove.

Terry had built an organization with the simple

affiliation of friends who share a common culture. In

organizing they were able to fend off attackers and become

a money-making force in the neighborhood. America had

led him into gangsterism. The mentality as it relates to the

environment where behavior was governed by codes which

dictate how respectable manhood is seized and maintained.

Deprivation in the black American culture dominates which

calls for the gangster lifestyle for him and his friends'

survival. Fueling the criminal behavior in the

neighborhood was the lack of good paying jobs for immigrants. Limited jobs led to the search for alternative illegitimate means to secure resources. The frustration of seeing parents' cyclical failures created a counterculture where masculinity was tempered by frustration and aggression.

Terry's father was not around, and no father oversight, led to neighborhoods seeing more and more street corner social networks that turned into criminogenic opportunities to secure a lifestyle more individualistic than family oriented. Neighborhood boys with similar plights gave rise to hustlers, pimps, pushers, and thugs. When running with the likes of these personalities it was important to have a code. This allowed for respect-loosely defined as being treated right or being granted one's props. The code allowed for the negotiating of respect. With the right amount of respect, no one could not just bother you in the street. If so, this would call for a disgrace for them or a diss, which was usually physical harm. The code of the street replaced the police or the judicial system for the Zoe of Miami.

Terry quickly learned that respect was an external entity, one that is hard-won but easily lost so he must constantly be guarded. The alienation a person can face from the mainstream allows for adaptation; and for poor inner-city blacks, this was just one of many keys. Learning the ways of the streets solidifies the reputation, which becomes social currency that yields the kind of fear and respect that is important for the survival in depressed neighborhoods. Terry's reputation in the streets was growing due to the moves he was making in the dope game and with the Zoe Pound in participating with the car shows.

Terry knew he would have to build a coalition among the peddlers in order to diminish competition for his product in the neighborhood. He decided the tactic of building an audience would be key in his plan. Terry would often watch the hustlers on South Beach play the tourists with shell games. The trick was using three identical shells to hide a ball and then rearranging them to pick where the ball ends up.

The hustler knew his audience which were the tourists. Terry would watch this scenario play out with one guy saying how bad the shell game hustler was and one guy actually winning bets. What others did not know was the hustler had two of his friends working with him. It was basically a sham game on the tourists. The mind state of tourists is that of having fun and spending vacation money for entertainment. The secret in this instance was to be in the right place and in front of the right people to facilitate your plan. One friend in the shell game would be allowed to win bets in order to lure people to play. The other would serve as a hype person to convince people that the game was legit. Unknowingly people would lose hundreds of dollars in bets.

Using this technique, Terry could use the Zoe Pound as a recruiter to congregate with street peddlers and distributers for the purpose of working together. As a cohesive group the Jack Boys could be minimized and ran out of town. Drive-by shootings and turf wars could be eliminated if all the hustlers were on the same accord. In essence this would mirror a corporate takeover in comparison to the business world. Terry knew this could eliminate the problem he had with Hollywood, and he also discerned that Hollywood's crew would not take this lying down. However many people supported Terry's vision, and this was the case of taking one poison over the other.

Terry researched and read books on various organizational models from the public library. He read silently to himself from one book titled the Prince. Princes who rise to power through their own skill and resources (their "virtue") rather than luck tend to have a hard time rising to the top, but once they reach the top they are very secure in their position. This is because they effectively

crush their opponents and earn great respect from everyone

else. Because they are strong and more self-sufficient, they

have to make fewer compromises with their allies.

Machiavelli writes that reforming an existing order is one

of the most dangerous and difficult things a prince can do.

Part of the reason is that people are naturally resistant to

change and reform.

Those who benefited from the old order will resist

change very fiercely. By contrast, those who can benefit

from the new order will be less fierce in their support,

because the new order is unfamiliar, and they are not

certain it will live up to its promises. Moreover, it is

impossible for the prince to satisfy everybody's

expectations. Inevitably, he will disappoint some of his

followers. Therefore, a prince must have the means to

force his supporters to keep supporting him even when they

start having second thoughts, otherwise he will lose his

power. Only armed prophets, like Moses, succeed in bringing lasting change. Machiavelli claims that Moses killed uncountable numbers of his own people in order to enforce his will. Machiavelli was not the first thinker to notice this pattern. Allan Gilbert wrote: "In wishing new laws and yet seeing danger in them Machiavelli was not himself an innovator," because this idea was traditional and could be found in Aristotle's writings. But Machiavelli went much further than any other author in his emphasis on this aim, and Gilbert associates Machiavelli's emphasis upon such drastic aims with the level of corruption to be found in Italy. Conquests by "criminal virtue" are ones in which the new prince secures his power through cruel, immoral deeds, such as the execution of political rivals. Machiavelli advises that a prince should carefully calculate all the wicked deeds he needs to do to secure his power, and then execute them all in one stroke, such that he need not commit any more wickedness for the rest of his reign.

In this way, his subjects will slowly forget his cruel deeds and his reputation can recover. Princes who fail to do this, who hesitate in their ruthlessness, find that their problems mushroom over time, and they are forced to commit wicked deeds throughout their reign. Thus, they continuously mar their reputations and alienate their people.

Machiavelli's case study is Agathocles of Syracuse. After Agathocles became Praetor of Syracuse, he called a meeting of the city's elite. At his signal, his soldiers killed all the senators and the wealthiest citizens, completely destroying the old oligarchy. He declared himself ruler with no opposition. So secure was his power that he could afford to absent himself to go off on military campaigns in Africa.

However, Machiavelli then strongly rebukes Agathocles, stating, "Yet one cannot call it virtue to kill one's citizens, betray one's friends, to be without faith, without mercy, without religion; these modes can enable one to acquire empire, but not glory. […] Nonetheless, his savage cruelty and inhumanity, together with his infinite crimes, do not permit him to be celebrated among the most excellent men. Thus, one cannot attribute to fortune or virtue what he achieved without either." Terry contemplated what he had read in the book.

He knew Hollywood was burning a lot of his bridges and connections in Carol City. He was robbing street corner peddlers and selling quarter keys of baking soda to other distributors. He was creating the rope that would sooner or later hang himself. This was essentially mobilizing his own hood in support of his overthrow.

Terry and the Zoe Pound maintained the White House as the central location for coordinating a lot of their activities. Everyone knew about the "White House" and if anyone planned to make a move on the crew it likely would happen at the White House. However, few knew that the White House was fortified with assault weapons and grenade launchers. Some of the boys from Hollywood's crew tried to do a drive-by on the Zoe Pound and were met with deadly force. All the members of Hollywood got shot but didn't die. Zoe Pound came out with AK-47s and spread up the car hitting each one of the drive by squad. They end up wrecking the car in the street and escaping North Miami on foot back to their hood.

Terry put word out in the street that Zoe Pound would retaliate against anyone that came at them. Terry knew he would need to keep tabs on Hollywood, and he knew he would have to deal with him eventually. He could not afford for Hollywood to dirty his name in the streets. He would use Hollywood's sister to reign him in.

Terry stood before a mirror in the "White House" and quoted from the book The Prince, "In addressing whether it is better to be loved or feared, Machiavelli writes, "The answer is that one would like to be both the one and the other; but because it is difficult to combine them, it is far safer to be feared than loved if you cannot be both." As Machiavelli asserts, commitments made in peace are not always kept in adversity; however, commitments made in fear are kept out of fear. Yet, a prince must ensure that he is not feared to the point of hatred, which is very possible.

This chapter is possibly the most well-known of the work, and it is important because of the reasoning behind Machiavelli's famous idea that it is better to be feared than loved – his justification is purely pragmatic; as he notes, "Men worry less about doing an injury to one who makes himself loved than to one who makes himself feared." Fear is simply a means to an end, and that end is security for the prince. The fear instilled should never be excessive, for that could be dangerous to the prince. Above all, Machiavelli argues, a prince should not interfere with the property of their subjects, their women, or the life of somebody without proper justification.

Regarding the troops of the prince, fear is absolutely necessary to keep a large garrison united, and a prince should not mind the thought of cruelty in that regard. For a prince who leads his own army, it is imperative for him to observe cruelty because that is the only way he can command his soldiers' absolute respect. Machiavelli compares two great military leaders: Hannibal and Scipio Africanus. Although Hannibal's army consisted of men of various races, they were never rebellious because they feared their leader. Machiavelli says this required "inhuman cruelty" which he refers to as a virtue. Scipio's men, on the other hand, were known for their mutiny and dissension, due to Scipio's "excessive mercy" – which was however a source of glory because he lived in a republic."

Chapter 8

Terry had many opportunities in expanding the Zoe Pound network and making more money on the streets. He used his network of contacts made while doing car shows throughout Dade County for promoting his product. He had been to dozens, if not hundreds of organized car shows in his life; many had been excellent, more have been adequate, and a fair few had been a little underwhelming. Part of the problem was familiarity. A local car show in the Miami area would inevitably attract the usual *culturally approved* American 'classics', which meant a preponderance of Chevy low riders, Convertibles and Caprices. Even E-Type Jaguars struggled to turn heads– park one next to a late '80s XJS and every show goer would be gawping at the buttressed underdog instead.

In many cases, the only difference between a car show and a car park was that the exhibits in the former were usually freshly polished. Their owners often stood by should you wish to ask a question. Prepare to be either locked into an unfathomably detailed tale about nut and bolt restoration, though, or to be disappointed by the very opposite – an owner who had bought his or her 'classic' just to gain access to the show circuit. Terry noticed this increasingly frequently of late, it seemed that fresh retirees were buying the cars of their youth and haven't necessarily topped up on the car 'knowledge' they built up forty years ago. Some didn't even seem particularly clued up about their own ride. Alas, these days, He seldom chatted to an owner unless the car particularly piqued his interest. He just tipped them a polite 'nice. Thanks' nod, and usually received a knowing smile in return.

At least expertise hadn't been in short supply at certain single-type events he had attended. Ford RS events took geekery to breaking point, in a thoroughly enjoyable way. At events like those, owners and onlookers alike seemed to have eyes calibrated in *thou* and an uncanny ability to identify carburetor upgrades, non-original stickers, and outright counterfeits. Impressing the RS guys ain't easy. Same with Saab people, Impreza fan boys and Mini lickers. Sometimes, a narrow scope of eligible models can be good news in other ways.

Young Haitians in the neighborhood began to see Terry as a type of savior for his people. He had established a reputation as an up-and-coming businessman. He was the only Haitian making tangible progress as a leader among the people. The Zoe Pound was viewed with fear and awe in the North Miami neighborhood. While the reputation of the crew was growing so was Terry's power and influence.

Terry had become a major player and the crew were branching out into other money-making ventures. Jean, Benny, and Jay Frank were becoming big time figures on the hustle scene. They all had their own underling followers. These younger guys would do favors for the crew just to get a reputation by affiliation. They would often be used because if they were arrested they would go to juvenile detention centers instead of prison. Many of these guys were second or third generation immigrant children. They had a greater knowledge of American culture as a tool against their less-informed mothers and fathers. They utilized this knowledge in manipulating their parents to get out of the house and hang in the streets.

While the crew's major business was slagging dope and robbing ships its young guns did hits in the hood. The work put in by the young want-a-be hustlers only added to the allure of the Zoe Pound image in the neighborhood. They made the Zoe Pound name infamous by becoming major enforcers on the streets for the crew. Many of the neighborhood youth knew the members and associates of the Zoe Pound. These were people that saw the rise of the crew and knew them when they had nothing in the hood. Some of the neighborhood viewed the pound in the lens of Robin Hood taking from the haves and giving back to the hood. Generally the elders and resident citizens viewed the pound as a neighborhood menace. The neighborhood crime watch kept tabs on all the movements of the crew in which they relayed to local police precincts.

Terry was moving major units of cocaine on the streets, and he was making big money for Zoe Pound. Terry had efficiently maintained his network of street peddlers who were locking down the corners of Carol City selling dope. Other hustlers had no choice but to respect the Zoe Pound in this instance. The crew had maintained the North Miami area and moved in on Carol City flooding the area with grade "A" powder.

Zoe Pound maintained relationships with the gangsters in Haiti and were well respected by the Colombians for their ability to move kilos. Often these gangster would tip Terry and the crew to various stash houses which held dope throughout the city. When dope gets smuggled through the network and reaches a given destination it gets warehoused. It's usually stocked away in a local resident or house in a given neighborhood. This

knowledge was sometimes relayed to the Zoe Pound and

the home invasion would be set in motion.

The home invasions were brutal and deadly. People

were tortured and homicides committed for maximum

compliance by victims. Doors were kicked in and homes

were ram-shackled as the perpetrators searched for dope

and money. This mode was another way for the gang to

make easy money and score free dope. Those being robbed

were criminals and they certainly would not go to law

enforcement for help.

Many of the dope smugglers have written off at

least half of their product to government seizure or theft.

They plan for such misfortunate happenings and stock more

than required upon smuggling ventures. Most of the drug

product can be recouped by cutting the pure amounts with

lesser chemicals such as baking soda. The baking soda

would lower the potency of the drug which gives the user a

high. The preference was for a more potent product which

kept a user returning to purchase more dope. Terry was not

personally involved with home invasions, and he focused

his skills more on administering street level activities. His

strengths were in coordinating and facilitating distribution

activities in the hood.

Many of the local dope kingpins were catching

charges under the newly created RICO Act. Terry feared

he could fall prey to this type of charge. This provides for

extended criminal penalties and a civil cause of action for

acts performed under an ongoing criminal organization. In

other words leaders of a syndicate to be tried for the crimes

which they ordered to others or assisted in doing crimes

will be liable.

Terry knew he had to find a way out of poverty the

legal way. He had small business interests he was working

on, but he needed a master plan. In comparison to other

hood drug dealers Terry viewed what he did as a type of

job. He knew that he could accumulate a certain amount of money and assets to start his own legitimate self-sustaining business. Most drug dealers possess unobserved characteristics, such as low levels of risk aversion, high levels of entrepreneurial ability, and a preference for autonomy, that are positively associated with future self-employment, thus providing indirect evidence that these entrepreneurial characteristics are important determinants of self-employment.

Terry knew he and others like him were past working on a job for another individual in the traditional sense. The risks tied to drug dealing involved risks associated with criminal prosecution and physical harm from being robbed. Dealers also face substantial risks in terms of lost profits from having merchandise confiscated by the police or stolen by muggers. Dealers also had to deal with getting set up or framed by police informants and other competing dealers.

Terry was now focusing on longevity in the game. He had to view the entire aspect of hustling dope as a game. The issue he was coming to grips with was how he could win the game. His thought process would be challenged if he continued down his current path and he was ready for the change. He would certainly need to play his cards close to his chest and not let no one know of his plan to get out the game. As the saying goes. One should never let the right hand know what the left hand is doing. This could lead to betrayal and other acts that could be detrimental. Terry would remain unreadable among his crew and the people close to him.

Terry took interest in how the dope smuggling operation worked. He asked question among his contacts and got close to their networks. In all the lavish parties he attended and late strip club indulgencies he listened. He learned of smugglers using tankers and tugboats that would deliver shipments to a network of private sailors throughout

Colombia to the Caribbean Islands for shipment to the states. Many of the loads were destined for the Chesapeake Bay, Cape Cod, and the Hamptons before the stop off in Miami. One person usually took over at the shoreline, jockeyed the trucks or vans, and ran the stash house. He turned over tons of dope in no time, sending waves of money washing across time zones. Teams of wheelmen, sailors and gophers got their share of the profits in the smuggling scheme. The gophers were any poor fellow who got talked into delivering a package or making a run. The gophers had the most dangerous part of the smuggling process. They could easily get body bagged if any product was lost or damaged during transport.

Terry learned that the key to smuggling was transportation. This sounded simple enough to the average law-abiding thinker. However, one must have access to a ship, airplane, submarine, or other transport to haul the product. There were hang out spots in St. Martin Bahamas or a Colombian port city for making contacts. Terry was told a potential smuggler could fly in find the nearest watering hole for tourists and make conversations. If no offer was made within a couple of days one could just find the nearest taxi driver make conversation and be put on. It was that simple. Basically be in the right place at the right time.

Terry had heard the stories of American smugglers caught slipping in these dope growing countries. Some dope kingpins had crematoriums in their lavish homes with pans of ash filling the filters. Drug dealers were treated like lame racehorses, shot, and done away with if their plane could not take off, their boat leaked or if their truck failed to start. The game players at this level were no joke and it was serious business in these areas. Terry knew that if he could have a good insight into the process of smuggling it would better his hustle game.

Chapter 9

In Carol City the dealer was both the outlaw and the

entrepreneur. As a big employer in the neighborhood, he

offers the jobs with good money and an array of work

positions. This gave way to an entrepreneurial spirit among the black and minority youth of the area. The top worker in Terry's organization could gross about $5,000 a week. This came along with wearing all the current fly gear, driving top of the line cars, eating at all the expensive restaurants, VIP status in clubs, strip bars and all the women one could have. Some positions Terry hire for were lookouts or transporters, holding nine to five jobs. Some were hired to go out west to buy guns, while some hired rented out their apartments as crack or stash houses.

Terry understood many of the elderly residents in the hood had moral repugnance for what hustlers do. They feared the violence and chaos brought in with dope and people getting hooked as users. At the same time the drug dealers and others employed were their sons, brothers, sisters, and friends. They could bring home food, medicine, expensive cars, and good times in a place where the finer things in life were rare.

Many of the youth Terry would put on were young boys and sometime girls. They would hustle after school at 4 to midnight getting money. They would give their parents excuses like they were at track practice or visiting friends. The parents would be slow to catch on that they had new clothes and shoes to wear to school. Many of the youth hustled to buy sneakers and treated their friends to expensive school lunches. The youths from the projects and single parent homes were especially susceptible to falling prey to dope peddling.

It was easy for a teenager to enter the drug business because he knew all the dealers in the hood. A new recruit was told where to station themselves and where the drugs was stashed. There were others that took care of the weapons or the police. Scramblers usually work eight-hour shifts and were paid weekly. These recruits often cleared about $400 dollar a week. Usually when they were busted by cops they would have no drugs on their person.

Terry had a number of captains on the block throughout Carol City and North Miami. These soldiers were not necessarily Zoe Pound members. They were more like Zoe Pound associates or workers. They were soldiers who came up through the ranks of hustling on the streets. One captain named Mel who was a good worker was busted at age 13 with $500 worth of dope money in his pockets. When asked by the cops what he was doing with the money he replied, 'None of your business.' He was immediately jailed.

Mel got 18 months of probation. These was typical for first time violators who had no previous arrest record. Mel completed probation and was back on the block. He was the youngest dealer on the block making $600 a week before he was busted by members of the Tactical Narcotics Team. Five officers whipped his ass so bad that after they caught him they let him go. He kept dealing. By the time Mel hit 15 he was clocking $700 dollars a week and had a

15-year-old pregnant girlfriend. With no education and no

real work history he was locked into the game.

Terry's main trap house netted as much as $50,000

a day. On the 1st of the month check day was the busiest.

There were hundreds of people coming thru a day buying

volumes of dope for recreational and medicinal use.

Repeat customers loved the especially potent dope and

were faithful repeat customers.

Terry's top earners walked around with $20,000 in

their pockets. Many wore bullet proof vests. The women

who came around, the cars, the cloths, and money earned

them unwanted attention and jealousy in the hood. Often

they were shot at, robbed, or kidnapped by shooters looking

for a quick score. They had to watch each other's back and

work as a team just for protection. Terry didn't have this

problem as a Zoe member. He had an immediate army

which could retaliate when called upon for action. The Zoe

Pound was vicious in the streets, and they exercised being

more violent than other crews. The Haitians had to push the narrative that American blacks had better think twice before trying a Zoe.

Zoe Pound members were expert at pulling heist on docked vessels at many of the various dock ramps throughout Miami. Terry once obtained a kilo of cocaine which was intercepted from a shipment from Peru valued at $2,000 in that country. That one kilo in the Mexican market was priced at $10,000 retail sale price. At wholesale in the U.S. it went for $30,000 on the market. In the hood Terry took the kilo and broke it down into grams to distribute. It easily grossed $100,000 within a week or two with workers going fulltime. Making money like this was more of an intoxicant than doing the drug itself.

Terry operated at the head of the Zoe Pound in coordinating the logistical network of dope throughout Miami Dade. It was important to move the product and any profits in secret, constantly maneuvering to avoid death or arrest. Terry depended on intelligent and loyal crew

member to play their role and do their tasks. Keeping

individuals well paid and acknowledging expertise over

various job functions were important in stoking egos.

Terry also developed the model of paying lower-

level workers in cocaine instead of cash. This move

allowed those who were ambitious to invest in their own

drugs. Those who were greedy hustled their own drugs and

were on the payroll for insuring Terry's supply reached

appropriate destinations for sale. In the dope game

handling people were very important. The slightest

insinuation of disrespect could ruin a person or operation.

People need to have some sort of connection to a cause and

Terry always sought a buy in inclusion strategy for

assigning job tasks.

Container ships from Haiti were always docked

along the Miami River and nine times out of ten they are

stocked with hidden dope. The trick is to being tipped off

to the hidden location of the contraband. Ships could be as vast as 180 feet and searching for product might be like searching for a needle in a haystack. Packages on these type of cargo ships could amount to totals of 310 parcels per load. This volume translates to about $9 million dollars on the streets of America. With this amount of money on the line a suave hustler could pay off police and dirty prosecutors. Terry rewarded the tipsters back in Haiti very well if information provided were fruitful.

While there was no identified leader of the Zoe Pound the inner crew recognized Terry as the head Zoe. This was apparent because he largely brought in the money for the crew. He had initiated all the move which made the pound a success in the hood. American blacks had no choice but to give the pound its props. Many longshoreman from the port of Miami were in Terry's pocket and although he didn't do business with them he obtained information. Most American hustlers dealt with the Port of Miami in moving work, but the Zoe had their own baby.

Terry would often ride out and go through the Matchbox or Flattops to get a feel off how the streets were in the hood. The rumors of dope movements were on the lips of fiends throughout the community. The Boobie shoot outs with Vonda was a normal occurrence. Other independent dealers had their own skirmishes on the block. No one wanted to fuck with the Zoes, and Terry wanted no unwarranted attention. With the closing of one of the major housing projects in Miami the Boobie boy clan had to make another move. Vonda's crew ran Liberty City, and it was known among the dealers that Boobie eyed this option.

Terry's crew maintained a number of weapons and they largely utilized AK47s for maximum fire power. The AK47 in 7.62x39mm and the later AK74 in 5.45x39mm are some of the world's most ubiquitous weapons. One of the biggest reasons for its use is that the AK series can be

fielded for a significantly reduced cost in comparison to

other systems. A basic AR-based system may run in excess

of $800 for the basic rifle, with accessories totaling several

hundred dollars more. Thus, many shooters find it

necessary to have more than $1,500 invested in their rifle

cache, a sum many fans find they simply cannot afford.

Completely useable AK series weapons from several

manufacturers can often be fielded new for less than $500

for the basic weapon with a slew of accessories similar to

those available for the AR-15 available at reasonable

prices.

While the AK series is relatively inexpensive—it is

not cheap. The weapon itself has been proven on every

battlefield on the planet. Just as with AR series weapons,

there are "tiers" of manufacturers. Some produce higher

quality weapons than others. With the AK series, most are

entirely serviceable, albeit some rougher than others, from

the start. With some of the AR-15 clones, this is unfortunately not always the case.

Carrying rifles allowed for the engagement of the enemy well beyond the range at which pistols, or shotguns are routinely considered effective. He didn't want his crew in on the warring factions. This largely resulted in negative publicity, unwanted death, and bad business. Let alone the army of cops and special task force agencies slinging around warrants. Finally with the robbers and head hitters waiting in the wings to pick over the dead carcasses the whole scene was a nightmare for the bosses.

Among thieves or criminals there was supposed to be a type of honor among them. However, in the Miami culture of dope dealing this was not the case. It was a dog-eat-dog world, and the prize went to the one with the balls to take it. Terry was numb to this culture, and he was not surprised with the war among dealers. He would purposely be prepared for the war that may precipitate in his backyard so to speak.

Terry knew as in The Prince, there should be no other objective, no other thought, nor take up any profession but that of war. He quoted to his minions, "The only thing a prince needs to study is the art of war. This is the primary discipline of the ruler. Mastery of this discipline can make even a common citizen a great ruler. The easiest way to lose a state is by neglecting the art of war. The best way to win a state is to be skilled in the art of war."

Chapter 10

South Beach maintained high profile Gucci shops,

unisex beauty and tanning salons, beach clothing outlets,

outdoor restaurants, and bars. Women from various

cultures walk the sidewalk with string bikini outfits and

Versace shades. European made cars line the streets from

Ferrari vehicles to Mercedes. Immigrants scuttle to work with their lunch bags wadding through the crowd of visiting tourists. As the ever-present crowds make their way up and down the street, the Heights seems a living embodiment of the American Dream – a vibrant, energetic urban melting pot.

Those oceans of tourist were oblivious to the Miami culture of Carol City just beyond the bridge that separates the island from the mainland. If tourists traveled to experience the Carol City culture of 1990's Miami they would see tough teen-agers wearing beepers. Youths with four-finger gold rings and $95 Nikes run the streets. On every block there are two to three crews touting its own brand of drugs and Terry wanted to control it all.

Terry was curious about the crack epidemic that was washing through the major cities in America. Crack was a form derived by free base or powdered cocaine cooked up under the flame of a fire. The drug had traveled up and down the east coast. In traveling to other cities for football games, national car shows and parties the drug was infamously known for making money. Terry theorized for every successful citizen or college graduate there are other who have dropped out of school, had a child out of marriage, become permanently unemployed are likely candidates for drug use. He knew by experience that drugs do best where Americans do worst.

Terry's crew had become seasoned hustlers. Dope dealing requires the ability to exercise quality control, hire a dependable workforce and develop steady clientele. They had become adept at putting teams together. Columbians were expert at smuggling and getting drugs logistically into the United States. The crews in Miami and other parts of America were experts at retailing drugs and customer service so to speak. They were the toast of many parties where mirrors sprinkled with powder and snorted through rolled up high denomination bills occurred.

Terry occasional partied on South Beach and he took note of its drug scene. On this scene they did more free base in comparison to drug use in the hood. There were more snorters on South Beach. They sought a more intense high through the act of freebasing. This involved treating cocaine powder with ether and reducing it to a crystalline base, which, when smoked, produced a sharp, pleasurable rush. Freebasing was complicated and messy, the subject of instruction booklets running on for many pages. Freebasing could often result in explosions which could badly burn a person.

Customers demanded that the product should come already prepared and cooked. This gave rise to the crack epidemic. Terry being the entrepreneur he was realized he could build an economic empire with this product. The new form of selling converted cocaine to freebase required a filler. As cocaine loses its weight in cooked form. Terry used baking soda which could be easily blended with cocaine and maintain its quality.

Zoe Pound members trained its street level hustlers on how to mix ounces of cocaine to be cooked up. Adding baking powder and boiling on a stove top combined the ingredients. Letting the substance cool into a solid mass and breaking into small pieces required a closely monitored work force. Well paid females were recruited to break the product up while in the nude. This was required to prevent against theft. In this packaged product it easily served up to 2,000 or more people.

Terry presided over a well-established network of retailers on the streets of Carol City. The crack product was poised to generate millions of dollars in sales. Crack would permeate the Miami Dade environment and become a cultural phenomenon in the community. Hustlers of all backgrounds worked as drug dealers and middlemen in making buys. The product especially hit the poor hard because it was an inexpensive drug. It got its name from

the crackling sound it made when smoked. It became easy

profit to cut the pure product with baking powder or other

filler for public sale. As many dealers became greedy this

often resulted in unfortunate deaths by overdosing.

Terry had made a few valuable contacts while

hanging out on South Beach. He met a New York hustler

named Raul who was of Dominican descent. He was a

major crack dealer with ties to the Cali Cartel in Colombia.

He invited Terry to hand out with him in New York and

arranged travel for the visit himself. Terry made the trip

and experienced firsthand how the northerners ran their

operation.

Raul's territory was the Washington Heights area,

the Upper West side of Manhattan. There were a lot of

bodegas, outlet cloths shops, farmacias all reminiscent of a

Caribbean bazaar. It seemed salsa music could be heard

coming from all the mom and pop stores. The streets were

packed with Irish, Jews and mostly Dominican people.

Raul was a slick talking hustler. He enjoyed telling

jokes and ribbing on the guys that served as his body

guards. He was a personal person who enjoyed

conversation and good company. He befriended Terry at a

South Beach night club and Terry saw value in him. He

thought he could learn something from his association with

him.

Raul's operation ran 24 hours a day, seven days a

week. Dealers set up shops across the street from schools,

enticing any they see with free samples. They offer two-

for-one deals and holiday specials timed to coincide with

1st of the month check payout days. Their marketing

worked so well they had customers looking for them.

Raul's operation fanned southward into Harlem and

eastward into South Bronx. The black Americans in

Harlem, South Jamaica Queens, and Brooklyn all hustled

Raul's product. The crews in Bushwick and Brownsville

made the most money selling crack. These cats were

hungry for money, as most of them were jobless,

uneducated, and broke. You could get fronted an ounce on

commission, make $1000 dollars pay it off and hustle the

rest for profit.

Terry compared Raul's organization to his own and

noted the close relationship they had with the Colombians.

The Cali Cartel was the second-largest syndicate after the

Medellin Cartel. Shipments were arriving in New York by

the ton.

The two groups got along well, and they both

shared the common tongue of Spanish. They both had an

entrepreneurial spirit coming from third world countries.

Raul was the main supplier for American blacks controlling

Harlem, Queens and Brooklyn and he dominated Upper

Manhattan and the South Bronx.

Terry hoped he could develop better relations with the old gangsters in Haiti and possibly mirror what Raul was doing in NY. He made the trip back to Miami with a new resolve and began strategizing a way to streamline the crack process in Carol City. If Heroin was the Fortune 500 club then crack would be the Mom and Pop bash. Other drugs were more controlled in the way they were distributed or sold. There was no order in crack and this posed array of additional unwanted problems. It was essentially a chaotic dog eat dog world in the crack game.

Terry would organize his crack selling team with no more than seven or eight people he could trust. He decided he would use Zoe Pound members to begin his infiltration into the streets of Carol City. He designated Benny as a street seller, Jean was the steer person who directed customers and Jay Frank served as guard for the merchandise. Benny used one of his do boys as a police lookout and Jay Frank chose one of his runners as a weigher or scale boy. Terry was the manager who would keep count of all profits. Terry essentially ran the coordination of two money making operations. The dope game was profitable, and the crack game was a new upstart with loads of potential. The Zoe Pound continued the primary business of pirating dock ships. They robbed incoming shipments and used the product to partly fund the crack hustle.

Crack created a new breed of urban guerrilla. Turf wars broke out over the most lucrative dope holes. Dealers began popping up to try to copy and compete with the Zoe Pound in sales. Dealers regularly ripped off customers and stole from one another. Shootouts, stabbings, and executions became prevalent in the community. The police were outnumbered and outgunned in comparison to the average crack dealer gangs. A lot of the dealers utilized the AR-15 weapon. The AR-15 is without a doubt one of the most ergonomic weapon designs to ever be fielded in large numbers. During a six-magazine endurance test by pawn shop sellers, which admittedly was not a true endurance test but rather a proof of ability test, all evaluators found that it was much easier to change magazines and get the weapon back into action quickly with the AR-15 design than other average designs used by law enforcement. Reloading is a key in any gun battle shoot out.

Chapter 11

Terry had his hands filled with running two drug organizations, managing the car club business, and robbing docked ships for dope. He had been thinking of Sheryl for weeks and had not seen her since he had returned from his trip to New York. Sheryl would have loved to have gone on that trip he thought to himself. She was the type of person who was curious about other cultures and how people lived. Sheryl knew that Terry hustled but she was unaware of the scope of his endeavors and what he had his hands in.

Terry invited Sheryl to an exclusive Italian restaurant in Brickell. He knew she enjoyed foods of various cultures. She was worldly when it came to things like that. She would often confide in him how she wanted to travel the world one day.

"I heard you were in New York," said Sheryl.

"It was for business," replied Terry.

The restaurant was styled with high ceilings and glass chandeliers. Ivory statues of grapevines lined the outer walkways with decorative mirrors on the wall. Chequered tablecloths covered ornate tables and beautifully patterned carpets covered the floors.

"You should have come with me, I know you like to travel," said Terry.

"I don't recall getting and invitation," replied Sheryl.

Terry smiled at her as the waiter placed appetizers on the table. Pepperoni Caprese Bites with Basil

Vinaigrette. This was an Italian Hors d oeuvre that Sheryl raved about often. Terry loved surprising her with treats. He enjoyed seeing the happiness in her face when she appreciated something. There were little pleasures for the dope pusher, and this was one of them.

"Listen, I want us to be serious with each other," said Terry.

"Serious how," replied Sheryl.

"I want you to be my girl," said Terry.

"I don't know about that, you seem like a player," said Sheryl.

Terry leaned back in his seat and sighed. He knew he had to convince her that he was a one-woman man. Having a playboy image was part of the dope game. It was a show and what people referred to as a flauge or fronting. Making the truth of who one really is to get along and manipulate others.

"Girl you know I've been after you for a long time," he shot back.

She smiled and he knew he had her. She was a logical person, and it was true that they were flirting with each other since first meeting. Her brother was largely the issue that stood between the two getting together.

"Let me think about it," she replied.

Terry knew he had her. However, he would play her game. They enjoyed a quiet dinner followed with desert. After dinner they strolled the Brickell courtyard district and walked along the intercostal waterway. A few other couples were out sitting on nearby park benches and enjoying the cool breeze off the waterway. The two held hands under the moon light as they strolled pass the towering buildings of Brickell Avenue.

Terry enjoyed moments like this with Sheryl. She made him feel normal and it gave him a grounded feeling. He did not have to play tough with her. He was free to be himself and express his inner feelings. Terry decided that night he wanted her company on a regular basis. He would ask her to move in with him. He had been planning to invest his money in a prosperous venture and what's more prosperous than real estate. He had been looking at various areas of Miami and was at a lost on where to go. Coral Gables was a nice ritzy area, but it was too far from his hood. He thought Brickell was too metropolitan. Terry liked the beach, and the perfect investment would be the Aventura area because of its access to the coast. Terry would consider making contacts for the purchase of a high-rise condominium on Aventura. This would be ideal for him as a place for his new life partner and a fresh start for becoming legitimate.

Terry sat on the balcony of his newly purchased high-rise condominium. He purchased it for $500,000 and it came fully decorated. It was the showroom model and because he paid it outright he got the best selection. Sheryl was smitten by the condo and agreed to move in without hesitation. This was the life she dreamed about as a littler girl in Carol City.

Terry had a number of stash boxes designed in his house for the storage of surplus cash. He usually used the White House and other safe houses maintained by the Zoe Pound. He decided to keep this secret from Sheryl as he knew her brothers were crooks. He hated keeping secrets but in his line of work this resulted in life-or-death situations. He always had an emergency stash of $20,000 and maintained about 1.2 million in a hidden safe. The rest of the money went back into the organizational functions and miscellanies payments to workers, parties, etc.

Terry attempted to maintain a regular social life outside the life of hustling and violence. He had ambitions of going legit. He needed to establish ordinary connections and do ordinary things in order to make such a move. He in a sense would need to separate himself from the day-today operations of his various ventures. Terry still had loose

ends out in the dope game and anything could happen on

the streets. He was unsure how to step out of the game.

Hollywood was still out there lurking about in the shadows

and his brother Aston was a lingering issue. He was unsure

if they were actively working together. He did not want to

bring Sheryl into the situation because I could possibly end

in a detrimental state of affairs.

Terry conducted all his business out of his place

of residence. Whatever he did in the streets was left in the

streets when home. He desired to have a safe haven away

from the block and privacy was vital. This prevented

against drive by shootings, kidnap attempts and

backstabbing set up attempts. He also sought to protect his

lady from the violence of the streets and cautioned her on

what she talked about with her family. He knew one day

she would be saddled with making the choice of them or

him.

Terry's business venture netted him millions of dollars in profit and coming into the mid-1990s translated to a good year. It was nearing a new millennium and law enforcement was conducting its war on drugs with guns blazing. The cultural blitz was hitting Miami like a hurricane and the drug wars raged on with the take down of the Cocaine cowboys. Law enforcements were giving away indictments like the candy lady in the hood. The three-strike law were putting dealers out of the game like tick tack toe.

Terry was well respected in the Carol City neighborhood and his name was good in North Miami among the youth. The residents of the community distained violence and the drug scene in the area. Many joined neighborhood watch groups and rallied with the just say no movement initiated by the government. Terry made it a point to give back to the community so to speak. He did school supply giveaways, Turkey drives for

Thanksgiving and Toy drives around Christmas. He helped the elderly with bills and paid people's light bills.

The Zoe Pound remained a vicious beast in the streets and earned its reputation as a major gang among gangs in Miami. Black American could not just push around Haitians like they did in the early days of immigrant settlement in the neighborhood. The Zoe reputation transcended covering all Haitians. Any Haitian was referred to as a Zoe in common street lingo. They were no longer a joke and were considered major players now.

Terry referred to the treatise the Art of War to his crew. He quoted, "The art of war is of vital importance. It is a matter of life and death, a road either to safety or to ruin. Hence it is a subject of inquiry which cannot be neglected. The art of war, then, is governed by five constant factors, to be considered in one's deliberations, when seeking to determine conditions. These are: Moral Law, Heaven, Earth, The Commander, Method, and discipline. The Moral Law is loyalty undismayed by danger, Heaven signifies time of day or season, Earth comprises open ground or chances of life or death, The Commander represents courage and strictness, Method and discipline encompasses proper marshaling of the army and resources to the cause."

Terry maintained control of his street level connections and he remained visible in the neighborhood. His mother continued to work in the hotel industry, and she was unaware of his notorious rep in the streets of North Miami. She knew of his car show business and was always of the opinion he was traveling due to business. Terry's friends and associates knew his mother was oblivious to his street activities. They made sure that no one messed with her and provided protection by keeping an eye on her house in the neighborhood. No enemy could retaliate against him by getting to his immediate family or relatives.

Chapter 12

Terry was hanging out at the local watering hole on South Beach called Wet and Willie. This was the spot where most African American tourists hung out when in Miami. A person was able to meet people from all over the country in this one spot. Terry sat smoking on a fine Cuban cigar while he viewed the scene of people talking, milling around, and having drinks at the bar. He had just left Carol City and decided to relax with a change of scenery. He noticed a group of women with this one guy taking shots at a nearby table. Terry sat alone as he munched on some wings and sipped his cold corona. As the group continued to drink they became rowdy and so as Terry finished his meal he walked out the bar to his blue Chevy Caprice parked Valet in front of the bar. The group exited following Terry and one of the females tried to engage him in conversation.

"Are you from here," the girl asked.

"Yeah, what's good," Terry replied.

"I'm from Carolina down with some friends and we're looking for some weed," she said.

"Yeah, you five o," said Terry.

"No," she replied.

"Cool, where are you guys staying at. I can bring you something later," said Terry.

Terry drove over to the Loews Hotel parking lot and sat in the lot tying up an ounce of weed in a zip lock. The female at the bar had given him the address and room number at the Lowes. He was familiar with the hotel from sponsoring parties he sometimes did for car show promotors. He made his way up to the room with the pot and knocked on the door. The door was opened by the guy that was at the bar with the females.

"Yo, come on in man I'm Slick," he said.

Terry entered and Slick led him into the T.V. room of the suite. The females sat around sipping on coolers and chatting about their experience on the beach. Terry took a

seat beside the girl he chatted with at the bar and dropped

the weed on the glass coffer table. Slick immediately

began rolling joints for the females. He pulled a knot from

his pocket and dropped it on the table in front of Terry. He

then lit a joint and passed it along to the girls. They all

began smoking and chatting as Terry look on. He had a

policy of not getting high on your on-supply motto. As he

sat Slick passed him a beer and chatted him up. Terry

found the group was from a small town in South Carolina

called Lake City. Terry got the impression that he was a

small-time hustler because of his swag. Slick was well

dressed in the newest gear. He sported black timberlands

with baggy Levi jeans. He wore an all-white Miami

Dolphins jersey with an oversized gold roped chain. The

curious thing about his gold chain was that it had a gold

pendent of a rose. Terry thought this was odd. Here sat

what seemed was a hardened street dude with a flower

around his neck.

Terry continued to chat with Slick and later found

out the Rose represented the name of his mother.

Apparently his mother had a big impression on his life, and

he explained how she always instilled in him the drive to

hustle for a better life. He was not in the game for the sake

of money or a name but instead to conquer. As he listened

to this man he could see a whole new view of America

from a rural native. South Carolina was considered geechie

country and the land of the Gullah folks. Terry as a Haitian

born American felt a weird type of connection to Slick's

status quo.

"Listen I got a connect that can make you a million

dollars," said Terry.

"Word, I'm game," replied Slick.

This would work perfect thought Terry. Here was a

person motivated by something entirely different than

money. Most of the cats he met in Miami or other cities were about women, money, or power. All the tapestries of floss and glitz was what drove most men he had personally known. There was something real about this Slick cat. Terry and Slick moved their conversation to the parking lot of the Loews. He didn't want to talk business around the girls as he didn't know what relationship Slick had with them. And again it was not wise to openly talk business in the company of a lot of strangers.

Going into business with Slick allowed Terry to expand his operation into South Carolina. This would allow for the growth of Zoe Pound movement increasing cash flow and influence. Slick explained that in SC crack was just beginning to catch on. He could buy a few ounces of cocaine, return home, convert it to crack, and sell the product for three or four times the Miami street price. Upon hearing this Terry was sold on the idea of setting up the framework to make that type of money.

He returned to Lake City with Slick, and they set up shop in a two-story house near an area the called the block. The block was a place where the blacks can go to get haircuts, patronize bars, restaurants and listen to soul music. Enough poor blacks coughed up enough $5 bills Slick ended up buying his mom a $150,000 home in the white folk section of town. The move was so profitable Terry traveled to Lake City frequently just to get away from Miami.

Within a year of Terry setting Slick up in business he had recruited 50 workers who moved product through the area. Lake City included many small towns within the county. These small towns were populated by middle class blacks and poor whites. They were making up to $100,000 a day in the country.

Slick's Lieutenant was Puerto Rican Reek. He managed the street level distribution network throughout Lake City. He functioned more in the role of enforcer.

Terry had met him on a few occasions when he was up visiting Slick. Puerto Rican Reek was 6'00'', 200lb guerilla. Slick rarely hung out and preferred the company of females. Puerto Rican Reek was flashy and was always on the scene in clubs and at local football games. He reveled being in the spotlight. He was the opposite of Slick and Terry. He was pathologically violent. People who crossed him were pistol-whipped, beaten with baseball bats, shot in the legs. One 16-year worker, suspected of cheating, was beaten unconscious with bats, scalded with boiling water, and suspended by a chain from the ceiling until he shit on himself.   Most of his workers came from the projects and they were known as the hitters.

Slick was a very good businessman, and he coordinated all the logistics for getting product to SC from the bottom. When couriers made trips they would rent a motel room and set up times for Puerto Rican Reek to make the pickup. Slick followed the law of supply and demand.

When he saw crack selling for $15 in a neighboring city he would adjust the price to $5 in his area. Slick had hustlers renting out people houses to sell crack.

Puerto Rican Reek's propensity for violence led to him taking advantage of Florida's lax gun laws. He soon started requesting Uzis and AR-13 assault rifles with deliveries. This of course led to increase shootings and killings in Lake City. While the money could be made in these rural areas everyone knew everyone. It was easy to get arrested in a conspiracy charge in Lake City and Slick was well aware of this. Other hustlers throughout the City and other areas got word how hard Slick's organization was rolling. They tried to compete by incorporating how Slick did business by recruiting out of town suppliers. It was basically no competition because he had already built a clientele and loyal customer base.

Terry could see that Slick was hungry and this made for an ambitious hustler that wouldn't accept failure.

Puerto Rican Reek was ambitious however he accomplished things in a different way. It was kind of like the good cop bad cop scenario. Both approaches were effective in getting things done but publicly one was palatable then the other. Terry could not look down on any aspect of how things were handled in the country. This was an entirely different environment, culture, and people with a whole different code of ethics.

Terry would've loved to see if Slick's business mind could've been successful in the Miami Dade culture. He would've liked to see how Puerto Rican Reek could influence a crew of Carol City hustlers and Zoe Pound killers. Terry would return to Miami with a refreshed way of viewing his environment and begin establishing his legacy. White flight transformed the surrounding neighborhoods of Miami Gardens. It was seen by black middle-class families as an attractive refuge from the Third-World streets of Overtown and Liberty City. By the

Mid – '80s, more than three-quarters of the neighborhood

was black and as the years passed, that proportion grew.

Terry would focus his interests on establishing a foothold

in Miami Gardens.

Miami Gardens property tax revenues plummeted to

the third lowest in the county, residents began blaming the

projects that was filling up in the neighborhood. The city

officials had set in place a policy of allowing low-income

housing to the detriment of the community. Terry would

seek to empower the downtrodden residents of the area to

earn work in the drug trade. Terry's ranks filled with high

school dropouts and floating criminals from the

neighboring Opa Locka neighborhood. Terry used the

streets to establish connections for funneling customers for

use of his product.

Chapter 13

Terry sat in the office of Sevilla Trading

Corporation with a suitcase filled with one-hundred-dollar

bills. The office was neatly furnished with modern chairs

and desks. There were a few employees chatting with

clients and couriers entered and exited the office in

intervals. The company sat in a leafy suburb of Miami.

Representatives took the suitcase and counted the money in

the back office of the building. They then delivered the

money to computer stores down the street. This was the

first step in cleaning money.

Twelve miles from the looming skyscrapers of

downtown Miami, drug kingpins had moved millions of

dollars in little-known maze of office parks. Terry learned

of places like this from his networking efforts on South

Beach. Networking is typically the best way to learn about

new opportunities. If one is not getting the results he or she

had hoped for by going out or hanging out with friends then

network. Terry was looking for new ideas and approaches.

So he had to step outside the box to get what he needed.

Terry discovered the drawback of earning or

spending money illicitly. It was hard to use this money for

legitimate purposes, except in small amounts. He knew if

he dropped large amounts of money on houses or in banks

it would demand a paper trail. He learned money could be

transferred as hard cash, diamonds, gold, cars, or an

electronic transfer. Electronic transfers were previously

preferred method of laundering. Associations with Casinos

were the best place to launder millions of dollars of hard

currency. Casinos generate millions of dollars a day and

it's taken to the bank with no questions asks. Such places

could simply pretend the millions were legitimate proceeds

from gamblers. So the casino cleans money turning dirty

money into clean currency.

Terry had no in route to the casino business, but he

did know how to get in on trading corporations. He knew

he would need to grease palms to get to the people who

could perform such services expertly without raising red

flags. Everyone was out to make a dollar in Miami, and it

didn't matter if it was illegal.

Terry learned corporations seeking to launder money had a totally different set of problems, and therefor very different methods. Nearly all business-to-business transactions were done electronically, moving digital currency from one bank account to another. This created a permanent record of the transaction, and so the transaction makes the operation seem legitimate.

Businesses need to account for every dollar earned and spent on their books. $10,000 bribe can't simply disappear from the books, it needs to be recorded as something seemingly legitimate and then the cash is used to pay the bribe. A company could account for whatever expenditure as payment to conspiring individuals or subsidiaries for services that were never done, or services that are vastly overbilled.

If Terry wanted to give an official a $10,000 bribe he could hire the services of a local attorney, accountant or consultant and pay him $11,000. The attorney gives

$10,000 to the official and keeps $1,000 for himself as a fee. There is a paper trail that displays payment for attorney fees. This satisfies any law or IRS requirement.

Terry was inspired to work with Sevilla Trading and had heard they were well respected in the market they operated in. He could use this in his step to become legitimate and possibly step away from the life of crime that ruled his world. Although he liked making money, secretly he sought the admiration from his mother in being a success and a credit to his kind. He had based all his beliefs in what others viewed as success and realized this was not his truth. He of course didn't want to be poor or a derelict. He had to adapt to the culture in which he was engulfed into. In coming from Haiti, a poor nation, he was cast into the rat race of the United States. He indeed adjusted in order to compete in the society. This made him the perceived monster that the public abhors in the minority community.

Terry knew he needed to do what he had to do to accomplish his dreams. He would need to do the dirt and reap the consequent adverse actions for the purpose of establish legitimacy.

Terry dealt exclusively with the Sevilla Trading Corporation executives, and they set up wired accounts for clients with investments such as computer stores. These executives were savvy in making investments and matching clients with accounts. It's difficult to determine money laundering when the actual person or entity is not part of the drug deal. So law enforcement would have a difficult time coming after the company in connection with a drug indictment.

Terry knew for most drug cases, the sentencing guidelines require a minimum of ten years to life in prison. The judge had no discretion to alter that. But the prosecutors do. So the only way to break that is by cooperating with them, by providing information that leads to the prosecution of other people. If you have a major

drug trafficker who is looking at 40 years in jail, and you

can get less than 6 years by negotiating, then that's a pretty

good outcome – much better than going to trail.

Terry found out early that it was good to deal with

high end individuals with connections. Although he

operated in illegal businesses he could reach out to

legitimate organizations who could held him. These were

people that knew the rules and how to operate within the

grey area of the law. The flip side is it's very expensive.

You can pay thousands of dollars just for information

which entails no physical work from the other entity.

Knowledge is truly power in this arena.

It was apparent that when it came to drug arrests

justice wasn't necessarily the top priority. Priority was

finding the major connect. For example, person X is

arrested with 40 Kilos in Dallas. The government wants to

find out who the people behind it are, which drug cartel is

behind it. It basically come down to associations. If your

high-end lawyer or representative is doing what they're

supposed to be doing, the offender is never the problem.

Offenders' values are packaged in a way to show their

usefulness to officials, and this is what generates

discussions or negotiations. This is how the well-

connected and rich operate in the real world. The poor are

not privy to these types of operations and those who

function as sheep will never understand this process. Only

the curious and those who dare to take a peep behind the

curtains will obtain the real truths.

One might say though that our present society has

been experiencing an increasing disparity between one end

of the scale and the other – with fewer in-between.

As an immigrant and former resident of Haiti Terry

was well aware of the situation of the "Haves" and the

"Have nots." In America money runs the society and those

with the most money have the most power. In Haiti the

government was known to strip wealth from the people by just taking of the country's treasury. In the United States this is done on more of a high level with legal and media centered complexity.

There has also been an incredible devolution with regards to political alignment and civility – which of itself is a separate topic. Terry could see many of the "Have nots" were being used to fuel the fire and were becoming meaner and dangerous. He could see this in the dope game. Young hungry and uneducated individuals whom inherent hundreds of thousands of dollars with no direction.

These individuals could possibly rise through the ranks of crime by the volition of their violent acts to run million-dollar organizations. With no conscience, no morals, or no compassion such individual wheel the power of life or death over multitudes of people. Terry had seen many monsters come to power in his time. The guys with the most power are usually the ones with the most debauchery associated with them. For instance the former

dictator of Haiti, Papa Doc, claimed to be a Haitian Voodoo

spirit. He also went as far as claiming deity status among

the people he ruled over as President for Life. It was said

he kept the head of one of his many enemies in the bottom

of his bedroom closet. It was also known that he watched

his men torture detained Haitians through peepholes carved

into walls. Individuals were tortured by submerging them

in baths of sulfuric acid and beat mercilessly with batons.

Terry himself did not see the need for merciless

violence and considered himself more of a businessman.

He sought to build a legacy and empire in order to get all

he could get from the game. He certainly was not

concerned with being the toughest gangster on the block.

Real recognize real and true gangsters acknowledges true

gangsters. Mobster's code of conduct has always been

based on three core values: secrecy, discipline, and respect.

In order to successfully navigate the streets one must

respect the rules. A true gangster will not be remembered

and celebrated for unnecessary killings or for being a rat

against your homies. Throughout all the streets and

playground of any hood was a major rule. That major

overriding rule was no snitching. Terry made sure to

school all his underlings with the rules of the streets. Many

of the rules came down to no talking to the police, no

stealing from family or homeboys, no disrespecting

homies, and no fooling around with the next man's girl.

Chapter 14

Terry sat at the White House in North Miami talking to members of the Zoe Pound about street business and hood rumors. He heard Hollywood had resurfaced and was trying to make moves on the street. He was trying to establish a dope hole or trap houses in the project area of Lucerne near the park. Hollywood had an established reputation in Caro City and was known as a hustler in the neighborhood. Terry had not heard much about his brother Aston. He dropped off the map since he and Terry parted ways from their dealings on the Port job.

It was rumored Hollywood arranged for the robbery of a member of the Thomas family. The Thomas ran much of their operation off of 183rd street and 27th Avenue. One of Hollywood's henchman had slapped a Thomas runner and held him at gun point robbing him of $40,000 worth of jewelry in the parking lot of a flea market. Members of the family was seeking payback for the slight and vowed to get back at Hollywood.

Hollywood had passed word to Sheryl of his interest in doing some business with Terry. However Terry knew that Hollywood was treacherous and could not be trusted from past dealings with him. His only link to Terry was through his sister and he continuously was blatant in his manipulation of her. Hollywood was looking to score some big money and he knew Terry was now a major player in the game. His robbing and thieving in the hood had amounted to chump change. Other crews were making money hand over fist dealing on every other block.

Terry's policy had always been to keep his enemies close to him. He weighed on the decision of fronting Hollywood some dope. Hollywood's crew was very efficient at peddling and turning profits. They also had no problems in collecting money and handling feuds in relation to hand-to-hand sales of dope in the hood. Terry knew that Hollywood's people could handle the work and they seemed hungry for it. He did not want any unwarranted wars among the crews peddling in the streets of Carol City. If he could pacify Hollywood and minimize beef in the neighborhood by fronting him he would. Terry notified the Zoe Pound to keep a tight surveillance on Hollywood.

Terry fronted Hollywood a kilo of cocaine from the insistence of his sister and Hollywood's crew went to work in the streets of Carol City. They set out selling $10 dollar bas of crack on the corner of the 35th Avenue and worked 24 hours a day. Hollywood's crew were intent on capitalizing on the crack-cocaine phenomena and required crew members to make individual investments of $1000 weekly for money to reinvest in the business.

Hollywood had his second in command collecting money and distributing crack cocaine to other street dealers outside of Caro City. They also attempted to takeover smaller dealers and merge them within their organization to expand sales. They essentially practiced hostile takeovers when competing crews refused to be absorbed. The group routinely offered rivals the ultimatum: "Get down or lay down." The choice amounted to joining the family or get murdered.

The Zoe Pound were aware of Hollywood's crew and Terry counted on his investment being doubled for profit. Hollywood would have to pay his debt soon and Terry would see if he would remain true to his word.

Hollywood's crew had a habit of showing off the trappings of their newly acquired wealth at a local haunt frequented by young people on Sundays - - The Tree,

located on 52nd Ave. Hollywood was known for his flashy

cars that included a drop top Chevy Impala with custom

Gucci interior. He and his boys rode the strip and played

loud music from big base bins setup on the street corners

for DJ battles.

It was later told to Terry that Hollywood's

organization was on the radar of law enforcement and had

been under its scope for about two years. Hollywood had

been named in a number of complaints by low level dealers

who were collared and arrested in frivolous stings

throughout the city. Law enforcements were aware of the

numerous robberies and the crews flaunting of exotic cars

driven in the hood.

Terry wasn't in a hurry to recoup from his

investment from Hollywood and he would watch in the

wings as things progress. He wanted no affiliation with the

crew as their time seemed up.

Terry found out through the grapevine that Hollywood's stash house was raided. The cops impounded four cars, two motorcycles, $350,000 cash, five semi-automatic weapons, furs, jewelry, 178 vials of crack and 3.5 pounds of powdered cocaine. It was discovered that Hollywood had amassed a mini-business empire within a couple of months. He owned 20 pieces of real estate and businesses. A few crew members owned Rim shops and auto-detail garages. Hollywood was busted the same day in as strip club on 62nd Avenue with an eight ball and two joints as he was driving out the parking lot.

Word was within a couple of hours he was back on the street checking his dope spots for cash payments and resupplying peddlers. This was a clear sign of snitching and collaboration with the pigs in identifying street dealers. His operation it seemed was not affected by the arrests and given renewed license to compete for business in the street.

Terry noted the first signs of snitching can stem from a "friend of a friend" scenario. Hollywood's sister was a major reason Terry considered dealing with him. He was suspect from the beginning and how he was a danger. Terry knew he would have to cut ties with him and there would be no more future transactions going forward with this guy.

In the meantime Hollywood continued to hustle with his crew and threw lavish parties in the hood. Hollywood knew he owed Terry about $30,000 for the front bestowed upon. It was well known in the streets how Hollywood was put back on. His treachery knew no bound, and he was never approached for the money. It was speculated that Hollywood was generating $17,000 a month in his dope endeavors. Members of the crew had been reinvesting in the business and it was apparent that Hollywood was spending most of the money. Members eventually began catching dope cases and getting convictions. One member was arrested for disorderly conduct, $19,000 was seized on his person and he received a 6-year sentence for conspiracy to sell crack. Another was caught on a weapons charge because of his former felony charge which he could not be around guns. With the team going down the money fell squarely in Hollywood's lap.

Terry sat in the barber's chair at the USA Flea market and observed the atmosphere as people got their haircut. His own barber was a black American who had cut his hair for ears, and he was also the owner of the shop. He was a square that had never been involved in the street life and was a family man. Terry imagined how peaceful his life must have been and wondered would he himself ever experience such serenity.

Barbershops were a local hangout in most historically black neighborhoods. Men come to talk about sports, politics or what's going on in the world. It was a good place to generate contacts, meet new people and learn who was who. He could also prospect for new recruits for his organization, so he did a lot of listening. People milled around for hours waiting to get their hair cut and chatted about worldly news. Boosters came in and out of the shop during the day trying to sell their acquired products to customers. As Terry enjoyed the bustle of the shop he closed his eyes while his barber trimmed his hair.

He listened to a group youth chat about various shot outs in different neighborhoods. He was well aware of the top-level hustlers and who ran which block or corner. There was a lot of talk about Hollywood's exploits and what he was up to in the hood. He was beginning to be held in the light of suspicion as his soldier were falling to arrest warrants and long prison sentences. Once a person gets labeled in the hood it's hard to get redeemed.

Terry attempted to operate with a kind of ethic. Street leaders and supporters know firsthand the value of ethical leadership that sets respect and the dignity of others as primary. Also many have witnessed the costs of wickedness and oppression. This is why Terry took ethics seriously. Because the importance of getting it right was primary.

Terry knew he had to make moves like a treacherous dude but not look the part. He always moved in a low-key way. He sought to project the low-key nonchalant persona and not attract a lot of attention to himself. People often were unaware that he was a Zoe Pound member and had most of the Carol City dope game sewed up. Only the people in the know knew who he was and how deadly he could be. People who knew what he was about had the impression that made it seem like he had protection at all times. No one really knew if he was actually alone or not. However no one was ready to test him to see.

In a crew certain members have the status of an O.G. or Original Gangster. This status is usually expected to provide advice, maintain harmony with the crew, and

provide protection of its members. Terry was perceived as

an O.G. and this status deters many aggressive advances for

the purpose of doing harm.

Chapter 15

Terry started the process of buying distressed properties in Carol City and acquired four crack houses. Usually a distressed property was any property whose owner defaulted on the mortgage on a home. Mostly commercial real estate and homes were distressed in a given area of the city. Terry determined real estate was a good way to spend his money because deals with distressed houses often require cash transactions. If he could become a good real estate developer this could transition him out of his life of crime.

Banks and lenders were usually looking to unload a property as fast as possible. So in this type of deal cash is a preferable source rather than financing. It also leaves room to negotiate deals if cash is readily available and accessible.

Deals are more successful and have a better chance when liquidated cash is on the table.

Terry canvassed the neighborhoods of Miami looking for homes that appeared to be in states of neglect or abandonment. He sometimes rode out at night to see what houses had lights turned off and seemed empty ready for sale. If he'd identify a house he would contact the buyer or realtor to make an offer for purchase. Terry thank got a home inspection for the property, got a lawyer to do a title examination to clear the title and got the paperwork to expedite the deal.

The process was long and arduous because of the extended waiting period. Often time paperwork had to be resubmitted and faxed to various offices. Once the property was secured Terry would make repairs and renovate certain sections of the house. Once renovation was complete Terry would turn would place the house on the market at a higher cost rate for a profit.

Terry would sometime keep some properties and rent them out to tenants for a residual flow of income to stream back to him. In addition, Terry did rent to own deals for individuals seeking to purchase family homes. He saw this as a way of giving back to the community in establishing stable neighborhoods. People did not have to worry about getting bank loans or problems with credit if Terry's company could provide ways to home ownership.

Terry saw that being a well-known and competent real estate developer could make for a permanent legacy. Regardless of your age, sphere of influence or net worth a legacy can be built. Every

personal interaction, written letter or recording adds to your body of work that will reverberate generationally through friends, family, co-workers, and associates. Terry realized this and wanted this rather than any material object on earth.

Terry had limited interactions with the Zoe Pound and the Carol City dope peddling worked as an automated process. The peddlers made the sales and were supplied with product on a regular basis. The distributions were automated process with drop off and pickups being conducted Zoe Pound lieutenants. Money was kicked upstairs to the bosses and split as required by agreed upon terms.

The Car shows generated little money on a sporadic basis. Cash prizes and bets were placed on the best detailed cars. Funds generated from patron entrance fees and cars entered into specific showcases were just enough to cover promotion costs. Terry eventually turned a few of his stash houses into living residences for rent. There was a steady flow of income coming in from these investments. Terry put this income on the books and began establishing credit to possibly be considered for future loans. He soon would be ready to start filing taxes and setting a base to make his jump from the life of crime.

Terry continued to do business transactions with Sevilla Trading, and he worked with building a platform to grow his real estate ventures. Sevilla had recently come under fire, and it was revealed in a probe that a number of institutions they dealt with were shell companies. Terry was slightly worried about such allegations because he was attempting to transition out of the game. He needed no unwarranted attention from governmental or law enforcement officials. He would complete he last transactions with them and make his move. However, Sevilla had been operating in the Miami Dade area for years and most of the organizations it dealt with were reputable major institutions. He insured his lawyers on retainer knew about and incorporated his real estate business transactions.

Terry set up most of his endeavors in his mother's name as to ensure it was protected against government seizure. He would actively control all of his interest, but legal ownership would fall to his relative. He desired to leave a legacy for his family and loved ones. He would do this with the right intentions and the legal way.

His mother was not aware of all the business interests Terry was involved in. She did know he was running the car shows throughout the city and of his investments in houses. She felt her son had achieved the American dream or success. Terry sought to shield her from his street life as he had learned what the real American dream was. It ultimately boiled down to power and wealth. With power comes respect and with wealth it creates opportunities. One must have money to make money and people with money like doing business with other people with money.

Terry had seen many great men who were leaders in their own right. They had come from all walks of life but had nothing when their time was up. Many competent leaders finish their journey without leaving behind much of a trace. It is beneficial to continue to change how people act or think in regard to establishing a legacy. Terry would seek to do this if it was the last thing he would ever create for himself.

Terry knew what mattered in life. He had the chance to experience many things from various viewpoints. He had experienced poverty and vulnerability. He had also experienced being wealthy and powerful. He had controlled the fates of many individuals as the overlord of Carol City and North Miami. He knew about team building and what it took to run an organization in a profitable way. These experiences had leg him to the knowing that loved ones were important.

Terry hoped to inspire others to raise and control their own fate as he did. When the surroundings control and dictate your wellbeing it's a defeat. Terry had learned to use his surroundings to accomplish his goals. He believed his experience could be key in solidifying his legacy for future youth in the community.

It takes tremendous willpower to turn off the cash and status water flow. Terry knew his time was nearing and he wanted to be prepared for the end. With many getting out of the game means a serious degradation in power, social status, and cash flow. This is largely an example of an outsized ego noted by many. Terry didn't have a problem with his ego. He felt the pull of freedom and valued it above all things.

Terry knew the backlash of this act would cause major ripples. There are powerful social pressures constraining any efforts to get out of the game. There are many friends and hangers on, to say nothing of extremely dangerous business partners, who have a significant interest in a person remaining in the game.

Terry had garnered a lot of unwanted attention from other hustlers in the streets. He had limited his contacts with his own crew. The Zoe Pound continued to deal drugs and make hits in the streets. Terry could see that he would have to make a decisive decision on his plans for the future. He would have to be masterful in his movements. He had grown the operations of the crew with the help of its core members. Jean, Benny, and Jay Frank grew up with him and had become boss players in their own movements. There was always someone waiting in the wings to take control of an organization once the top person goes down.

Terry had thousands of liquid cash stashed throughout his stash houses in the hood. He had money invested in his business endeavors and personal safes full of cash at his home in the suburbs. He continued laundering all the money he could in transition to realizing his plan. The car show business continued to be the central activity that tied the core founders together. They all attended and participated in events throughout the city. It was not tied to any illegal activities and was basically a legit activity. It was a community event that pulled together people from various parts of the city and all neighborhoods. Terry would have to step away from these social events in order to completely curtail affiliations with the Zoe Pound.

It was a daunting task to trace the origins of any deposit when there were about 700,000 global wire transfers occurring every day. Which is dirty money, and which is the clean money? Within the United States, the two primary methods employed by the government to detect and combat money laundering: legislation and law enforcement. Terry would make all the necessary steps to avoid persecution by the laws of America.

Chapter 16

Terry arrived at the White House around midnight

and the neighborhood was teaming with people on the

street because of the Haitian Flag Day celebrations. Many

specifically in the North Miami neighborhood celebrate in

remembrance of revolutionary heroes like Toussaint

L'Ouverture and Jean Jacques Dessalines and the

significant contributions Haiti had made to world history.

Jean, Benny, and Jay Frank were at the White

House overseeing the breakdown of a recent delivery of

bricks of cocaine. They all were unaware of Terry's

intention of getting out of the game and going legit. They

all were active with their own crew of homeboys, and it had

been some time that they were all together at once.

"Man we need another mission to go on," said

Benny.

"You mean jack another ship," replied Jean.

Terry walked over to the counter and poured a glass of cognac. Jay Frank watched him for a reaction to what Benny and Jean were talking about. Terry listened to the two and swirled his cognac in the glass as he sipped it. He could use the extra money for what he had planned, and the venture would mollify the crew for period of time.

"Why not, let's do the damn thing," said Terry.

"I can check with my source and find out when the next shipment," said Benny.

Benny's source was in contact with the old gangsters in Haiti and they were connected to the Colombian smugglers. Haiti had secured its place on the underground conveyor belt feeding Colombian cocaine to the United States. Many Colombian smugglers were casting eyes around the Caribbean looking for routes to pass product. Haiti with its instable political system, biblical poverty and bribe-hungry officials made it the perfect waystation. Many of Benny's connections were associated with the Jacques Ketant crew. Ketant stocked his criminal enterprise with brothers, cousins, and brothers-in-law.

Ties were forged between Haiti and the United States in this way among the Haitian expats in Little Haiti and other parts of Miami.

Zoe Pound got word that a freighter from Haiti was docked at the pier. It was believed that units of kilos were stashed throughout the hull of the ship. It was projected that the shipment was worth millions of dollars on the street. The pound assembled in a parking lot along the Miami River and prepared to board the vessel. They were all dressed in black with black hoodies, ski masks, gloves, and boots. Jean and Benny held the long rifle choppers. Terry and Jay Frank had glocks. It was pitch dark except for the lights shining from the ship. The men slipped onto the pier and snuck under the cover of the ship's shadows onto the bay.

Benny instantly rounded up the crew into the mess hall while the other men searched the ship room to room. The units were found in the bottom of the vessel's storage room wrapped and stuffed in coffee barrels. Terry, Jay Frank, and Jean loaded the product into large duffle bags slung them across their backs as they exited the ships. Benny had bound and gagged the crew and was waiting in the idling van in the lot.

The heist was successful, and the crew used one of the stash houses located in Carol City to process the take. Zoe Pound had successfully robbed the ship of 27 Kilos and would sell this on to local dealers at a rate of $17,000 per kilo. The pound would usually split profits among the original members which was a four-way split. The net profit was almost a half a million dollars and each member was looking at over a hundred thousand a piece.

Each founding member would have enough funds to put into their own network. They would in turn grow their network, invest in a business, or spend it on material things. Each person was empowered to make their own moves on the streets. Terry had mapped out his plan and did not feel the guilt of breaking away from the friends he had built an empire with. He felt they all took advantage of an opportunity and that opportunity had led them to financial empowerment. Terry would sell kilos to a selected few of drug dealers who were known. He would need to be careful and not sell to an undercover agent which were becoming prevalent in the hood.

Sheryl had been pressing Terry to put her brother on by fronting him some work for his crew in Carol City. Terry was hesitant to become involved with Hollywood again. He had a troubled relationship with him and his brother Aston. Terry dreaded giving him dope on loan for payment later. If Hollywood crossed him he would have to take drastic actions and he didn't want to kill anyone.

Hollywood and Aston had played a fundamental role in Terry's development in the dope game while in Carol City. Terry had moved on to organize his own kind to form the Zoe Pound and had become a force to contend with in Miami. It was unsure if Hollywood and Aston resented Terry's position with the Zoes. Terry was under Hollywood's tutelage and Aston had worked with him in early deals. Terry now basically outranked them on the streets and the Zoe Pound was a major player in the hood.

Hollywood liked to rent fancy rides. He partied in style racking up $180,000 tabs at the Fontainebleau hotel and its LIV nightclub. He rolled around the city with armed bodyguards and spent lavishly on jewelry. He was ostentatious and brash. He was well known on the streets and could move many amounts of units in short time spans. This quality was the only attractive aspect of Hollywood, and this is what made Terry consider him in moving product.

Terry reached out through Sheryl and word got to the brothers about a proposal to move a couple of kilos on consignment. In past dealings with Hollywood his work ethic was sound and his network in the street was vast. He had the regular street peddlers on the corners and the lookouts that warned of any police activity in the streets. In addition he had the freelance pushers that hung around nightclubs and bars. The freelancers partied with club goers for the purpose of establishing relationships. They then would infiltrate friendship rings and establish new clientele just from networking. This approach was ideal because you were able to sell to people with jobs and who were established income producers. His focus was not just crackhead and baser type people but the average working square.

Terry had not had contact with Aston for years and he played a major role in setting Terry on the path he was on. Terry had always wondered if Aston was secretly manipulating him at the behest of his brother. He was not able to actually substantiate that theory, but it didn't help when he suddenly stopped coming around. Aston did not display any signs of discontent or anger about anything.

From the experience of dealing with Americans in school Terry had learned to read people very well. He knew the classic signs of disgruntled individuals. Some people are friends with you because of what you can do for them. Red flags include friends who repeatedly try to sell you something, ask to borrow money again and again, or keep tabs on favors. These friends routinely cross the line between friendship and business.

In addition, manipulation, fundamentally, is managing the emotions of others, and not in a good way. It's sulking to get someone to feel bad, it's being especially nice to butter someone up. It's really hard to put your finger on whether or not it's happening, because being the target of manipulation is like being the proverbial frog in the slowly boiling water – it's only after you're out that you

realize the full extent of what was happening.

Sheryl and Terry were now living together.

Hollywood had always harbored disdain for the

relationship Terry had with his sister. When they were

younger he would sabotage any attempt for them to date

each other. She now served a mediator between the two

which could possibly resolve the long-standing contempt.

Terry however was distrustful of the brothers as they were

treacherous with their dealings on the street. There were

stories of them ripping off their own hustlers and robbing

suppliers. Such activities led to street wars and unrest in

the neighborhoods. Terry abhorred attention and any

unwarranted problems called the attention of the alphabet

boys. Terry had managed to operate below the radar of law

enforcement his entire criminal career. Many he knew had

caught charges and served time for criminal operations. He

would need to steer clear of law enforcement to realize his goal of exiting the game.

Traffickers often want to quit, but their divided self-identities make it difficult to relinquish the power and exhilaration they derive from the drug game. Harm reduction policies are needed that address the embeddedness of trafficker identities in dense webs of family, community, street gangs and transnational cartels, and the larger society, as well as the seductive appeal of Hollywood and pro-cartel narco-media. Traffickers need pathways that allow them to exit the illicit drugs business without surrendering their identity. Prison sentences are not enough to encourage traffickers to stop-also needed are culturally sensitive polices that help traffickers get out of the game and stay out. Terry was not fearful of prison but of losing his identity under imprisoned circumstances.

Chapter 17

Terry knew from reading newspapers that cocaine

came from a natural plant grown deep in the jungles of

South America. It was said to bear fruit, farmers' plant the

plant that make cocaine; then the plant is picked and

processed for distribution. The shimmering white colored

powder cross over transnational borders and eventually find

its way around the world where hordes of users sniffed it

up into someone's sniffing nose or shot into a user's vein.

Cocaine can either make you poor and weak, make you do

the unimaginable, make you wealthy - - or it can even take

your mind on weird trips.

Terry had never tried the drug, but he had heard

Hollywood got high on his own supply. He never knew the

rumor as fact, but it was common talk in the streets. This

made it harder in his contemplation of doing business with

the brothers. In the end he arranged a meeting with

Hollywood and Aston. They met up at the White House

and the two were not alone. They introduced Terry to this

kid named Fritz.

Fritz was a Colombian dude. He had gotten down

with Hollywood's crew and worked mainly as an enforcer

for him. He wasn't known for selling drugs and things, but

he was always on the scene with Hollywood. Terry didn't

know much about Hollywood's crew, and he wasn't

suspicious in the least about Fritz. Aston had vouched for

Fritz and with him cosigning Terry took him as just another

one of Hollywood's goons.

Terry and Hollywood planned for him to pick up

five kilos of cocaine. He was to make the pickup at the

poke and bean projects. The projects were a vibrant area,

and the neighborhood was a cultural mix of American

blacks and Cubans. Many of the youths there wore four-

finger gold rings, $100 dollar Nikes and Lee jeans. The

smell of curry chicken and fried conch from the kitchens of

the residents always saturated the air. Terry thought this

would be an ideal place for the transaction because of the

visibility and safety in numbers. Terry set the transaction

for midnight because the projects practically was live 24

hours a day. By the time the sun went down the night life

began for the neighborhood street walkers.

Terry had heard about how Hollywood ran his organization. His crew hustled crack for $3 a vial throughout 120 locations in the city. Out on the street poor young blacks – jobless, uneducated, and desperate – hungered for a piece of the pie that crack offered. To get started, it took as little as an ounce of cocaine, an investment of perhaps $1,000.

Cubans in Miami largely served as middlemen to the Cali Cartel and the Medellin Cartel. Hollywood in past dealing had conducted most of his business with the Cali Cartel through Cuban intermediaries. Terry learned that Aston now served as Hollywood's lieutenant and worked the local dealers in hustling crack.

Terry went to the extremes in validating Hollywood's street credibility, however he didn't trust the man. His inner voice was telling his something wasn't right. But he needed to get this deal done and unload the kilos he possessed. He loaded the kilos into the trunk of his

Chevy Caprice and drove it to the projects. As he waited

he contemplated his situation and looked forward to

making the extra money to get away. He checked his glock

to insure it was loaded and pushed it into the hidden holster

in his pants.

Benny had his crew working out of the poke and

bean projects. He had his crew meet up with Terry for the

transaction. The all sat in Terry's car as they were

approached by Hollywood and Fritz.

"Terry Mack, what you got for me homie," said

Hollywood.

"You got that bag," replied Terry.

Hollywood opened a leather Gucci bag he carried,

and Terry could see it was filled with money. He popped

the trunk and Fritz checked the package. Benny's crew

was uneasy about the entire exchange, and they were ready

for any surprise.

"It's good," said Fritz.

He took the satchel of dope from the trunk and walked

toward the front of the vehicle displaying the bag to

Hollywood. Terry noticed Aston was nowhere in sight and

this set off his silent alarms triggering his adrenaline.

"Freeze," said Fritz.

He put the nozzle of a 38 snub nosed pistol against

Terry's temple. The doors flew open on the Caprice as

Benny's crew sprinted from the vehicle. As Terry raised

his hands to show that his hands were empty he could see

Hollywood running through the projects. The projects lite

up with blue and red revolving lights. Black sedans pulled

up alongside Terry's Caprice followed by the blue and

white city cars.

Terry realized that he was caught. He understood

his run in the dope game had come to an end and his dream

of getting out was just that a dream. As he sat in the back

of a squad car handcuffed and defeated he wondered how it

had come to this. He was spirited off to jail and was locked

in a cell to await court proceedings.

The arresting officers soon realized they had

arrested a big fish and had identified Terry as a founding

member of the Zoe Pound. Terry was no rat, and he knew

the code of the streets. He was a true gangster and adhered

to the commandments of the dope game. He told the

alphabet boys no information, and they soon pegged him as

being the leader of the Zoe Pound gang. The media had a

field day with this determination and press was nationwide

of his arrest.

One of the major media magazine outlets wanted an

interview with Terry and this was granted by the State

Attorney's Office. They had hoped it would gleam some

additional detailed information of the Zoe Pound gang and

the drug network of Miami. Terry was sure that

Hollywood had set him up and he hated himself for falling

prey to his treachery. He sulked in his cell as he awaited

his fate for his perceived crimes. He had money stashed away and considered making outside contact to possibly get bailed out of jail. He didn't want to involve his mother and he readily removed the thought from his mind of contacting her. Terry's jail garbs were taken away and he was given civilian clothes for his interview with XL magazine. He's led to a jailhouse conference room with plain furniture and white walls. A scholarly looking white woman sat with her hair pinned up in a bun. She was surrounded by makeup people and cameras were set up at different positions around the room.

Terry entered and sat across from the woman. She began the interview by asking his name and where he was from.

"Do you know that you're facing federal charges for cocaine conspiracy & CCE," she said.

"No, that's new to me," said Terry.

She continued on listing the proposed charges the government had against Terry. She went on to talk about the others charged with him. She talked about his Haitian background and inquired about the formation of the Zoe Pound. Terry answered most of her questions, but he was careful not to reveal vital information could be used against him. Terry inquired of her details of his case and how strong the government's charges were against him. She ended the interview and spoke privately with Terry and relayed to him that he had a strong case for entrapment. She said the government placed an agent undercover to make the bust.

Terry returned to his cell, and he contemplated the conversation with the reporter. The only person he was unfamiliar with who had gotten close to him was Fritz. Frtiz must have been the agent that infiltrated Hollywood's crew. Terry wondered how long was Fritz working with Hollywood and who vetted him. Who vouched for his street cred and what was his link to Hollywood. He thought of Aston and Sheryl. Terry laid on his bunk thinking about his predicament and how he would explain this to his mom. He knew he would have to reach out and find someone to contact her. She would need to be informed on what was going on. He knew she would attempt to bond him out and find legal representation for him. However, he had money and could do it all without her using her own funds.

Once an individual is arrested on filed charges, the individual will be held in jail until his or her first court appearance. However, most warrants for arrest will include a bond amount and bond conditions. An individual can post bond, also known as bail, and be released to wait for their first court date. A bond is a peculiar agreement between the Court, defendant, and possibly a third party.

A bond is essentially a contract with the Court to attend all future court dates. The arrangement is very similar to a contract with a pawn shop. In a basic pawn agreement, a person places property in the hands of the pawn dealer in exchange for a short-term loan. Fail to pay the loan, and the pawned property is lost; that is how the pawn dealer ensures the debt will be paid. Bonding out of custody is very similar. The defendant is making a promise that they will appear for court dates going forward, and the loan is "secured" by a payment of cash or through a bond agent's guarantee of payment.

Chapter 18

For the years he spent in the United States Terry

never became a U.S. citizen, and now the government was

preparing a deportation order to send him back to Haiti.

Terry spent a year in a Miami Dade county jail and

indictment charges had not stuck. His lawyer successfully

used the entrapment defense and the government responded

with conducting deportation proceedings. Terry had not

worked with the government in investigating the Zoe

Pound. He now faced being sent to a country he knew

nothing about.

Haiti was identified as one of the poorest countries

in the world, according to the World Bank, with a G.D.P.

per capita of $846. Fifty-nine percent of Haitians live

under the national poverty line of $2.41 a day. Economic growth was low, and political strife was constant. The State Department continually advised against U.S. citizens traveling to the country. Terry dreaded the feelings of being relegated this fate.

It was said that houses are powered with electricity only a few hours every day, and that was if you were among the lucky ones. In addition, under the Duvalier regime many went without electricity and running water. It was believed that Haiti had barely advanced much since the days of dictatorship in the country.

Terry had remembered the stories from his mother of Port-au-Prince. The bustling Iron Market, the Port-au-Prince Cemetery, a warren of snaking pathways around built-up tombs, and the metal works area in neighboring Croix des Bouquets, where for generations Haitians have transformed the tops of oil drums and other pieces of metal into ornate masterpieces.

If you are a noncitizen of the U.S. and you have been convicted of a crime – nearly any crime - -there's a serious possibility that you could be removed from the United States. This is true whether or not you are here in lawful status. You might hold a valid visa, or even be a lawful permanent resident, but you can still be deported for a crime. In addition, if you're not in lawful status in the U.S., you can of course be deported on that basis alone.

Terry was transferred to a detention facility in Alabama by immigration authorities. He was bussed across the state and set up in his new facility. Investigating officials made it clear to Terry that their focus was on identifying, arresting, and removing public safety threats, such as convicted criminal aliens and gang members.

Terry was devastated with what the government was trying to do to him. He had spent his life fighting poverty and now they were attempting to send him back into it. However, Terry had one thing that could serve him

well as a tool. His experience had been vast and varied.
He could possibly use what he had learned in America to
empower himself and others in Haiti.

Terry was assigned a roommate at the detention
center. Andre was a native of Jamaica and he was being
deported after serving six years in San Quentin prison in
California for a robbery charge. Andre was a slim twenty
something year old dude. He had long dreadlocks and was
of a quick-witted personality. He was also the local drug
dealer for the in-house detainees waiting to be deported out
of the States. He had heard of Terry before he was
assigned as a roommate and was enthralled upon meeting
him for the first time.

"Man you gonna love it here," said Andre, "I'm the
man in this joint."

"I doubt it," Terry replied, "Man, I just passing
through."

"I'm gonna lookout for you, roomie," said Andre, "I want you to school me on growing my operation here."

Andre sold heroin to the detainees of the compound. A gram of heroin in Miami was running at a rate of about $80 and the price in prison was $400. Heroin made way within the complex walls in three ways: contact visits, mail scams, and guards smuggling it in. Andre revealed to Terry that he was bringing in 9 grams of heroin a week. He had a girlfriend that brought the dope in by stuffing a tampon and taping it under the visitation room seat. An inmate assigned to cleaning the visitation room would recover the stuffed tampon and take a spilt for helping smuggle it in.

Terry made it clear to his new roommate that he was out of the game. He said he would not help Andre sell drugs or take any gifts from him. He relayed this to Andre's clientele and other detainees of the facility. He did suggest to Andre that he should recruit mules. Get multiple females of his interest to come visit. Start by slipping a piece of candy in their mouth upon kissing. After a couple of visits this will become routine. Then one day at visiting concoct a story saying you owe a debt. I need you to bring some weed in that your brother has for you. When asked how just remind them how you've been slipping the candy into her mouth when you kiss. You can have someone on the outside wrap it in balloons and on visit time she slip in your mouth. You should swallow it to avoid detection and shit it out at a later date.

Andre took Terry's advice and implemented the plain. He used his girlfriend as well as other females he met through writing letters and other inmates' girlfriends. He soon was making as much as $5k per month. He was grateful for the instruction provided by Terry and set him up in a cigarette selling operation.

Terry had made it clear he did not want any reward from Andre. However this was a legal operation and he readily accepted it. He was a natural salesman and he sold

Newport smokes for $25 a pop. His customer base rapidly increased and he became well known in the compound as the man to buy from for smokes. This made the time go by faster in lockup and it also took his mind off his former life on the outside.

Terry had discovered an entire underground currency market in prison and learned to turn prison money into free world money. The currency used to buy pretty much anything in prison was a book of stamps. Postal stamps went for about six dollars a book. Convicts would send the money out from their commissary account or get their girl to do a street transaction. Money was also passed in the visiting room. Guys would keister the bills. To do this they would have to make a plug. A plug, was normally wrapped in Saran wrap and inserted into a condom and then lubed up, pushed up the keister or rectum until you are in the visiting room where you can remove it and pass it off to your visitor.

Terry found out that it was just as easy to get high in jail as it was on the outside. Many of the detainees used marijuana, alcohol, and heroin. It was said that anyone that ever served a significant amount of time knows that getting out of your head is an indispensable part of keeping your sanity. Terry's new product was now Newports. Terry now used his skills on his newfound product. He applied the crack commandments to his endeavor. If you're selling you have to be careful and have some willpower, or you'll use up all your supply you're supposed to sell with smoking with your celly. This could be the downfall of your whole operation.

Terry now understood to be weary of cell searches. All federal prison guards that are assigned to inmate housing units are instructed to shakedown several cells during each shift. This usually occurred while the inmate population was eating, though it could occur at any time. During shakedowns the unit officer enters the cell and pokes around for a few minutes. Some might only go into the cell and ensure that it's clean or doesn't smell of alcohol, while others elect to go through the lockers, any hanging bags, and do a more thorough examination. Other guards don't bother to search at all.

Terry had sparse contact with the outside as he awaited his fate and the process of the deportation system. His friends originally put money on his books weekly but that had dwindled as everyone got on with living their lives. His contact with Sheryl had become strained because of the issue with her brothers. He discovered she had moved out of their old place as she could not maintain the mortgage payments. He was happy that he had picked up the cigarette hustle as it allowed him to make enough money for some level of comfort. He lay slumped on his bunk puffing from a nub of a Newport. It had burned down and was now on the verge of burning out at the filter. He contemplated what it would be like in Haiti. He had not been there since leaving as a youth. Haiti was less than two

hours from Miami, and he was not inclined to visit the

place while in Florida. He now had developed a new bad

habit in lockup, smoking.